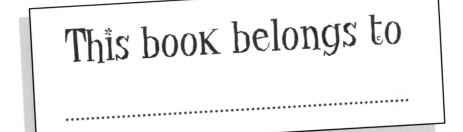

This book belongs to

....

50 SCARY
Fairy Tales

Compiled by Vic Parker

Sandy Creek
NEW YORK

An Imprint of Sterling Publishing
387 Park Avenue South
New York, NY 10016

ISBN 978-1-4351-4984-7

ACKNOWLEDGMENTS

The publishers would like to thank the following artists who have contributed to this book:
Advocate Art: Luke Finlayson
The Bright Agency: Si Clark, Peter Cottrill, Gerald Kelley, Duncan Smith

All other artwork from the Miles Kelly Artwork Bank

The publishers would like to thank the following source for the use of their photographs:
iStockphoto.com, Shutterstock.com page decorations alarik, dmiskv, Ensuper,
Eugene Ivanov, Hal_P, hugolacasse, Ints Vikmanis, lejlek, mariait

Every effort has been made to acknowledge the source and copyright holder of each picture.

Miles Kelly Publishing apologizes for any unintentional errors or omissions.

Made with paper from a sustainable forest
Manufactured in China
Lot #:
2 4 6 8 10 9 7 5 3 1
08/13

CONTENTS

HORRIBLE HAGS AND WICKED WARLOCKS

DARING DEEDS AND RECKLESS RESCUES

LITTLE VILLAINS AND EVIL MONSTERS

DOOM AND DEATH

BAD BEASTIES

Horrible Hags and Wicked Warlocks

The Witch

A Russian fairy tale, based on the Baba Yaga folk story, from Andrew Lang's *Yellow Fairy Book*

ONCE UPON A TIME there was a peasant whose wife died, leaving him with twins—a boy and a girl. For some years the poor man cared for the children as best he could, but at last he married again. However, the twins' new stepmother was very cruel to them and beat them and half starved them. All day she thought of nothing but how she could get rid of them. At last an evil idea came to her, and one morning she said to them, "I am going to send you to visit my granny, who lives in a dear little hut in the wood. You will have to work hard for her, but she will take good care of you."

The Witch

So the children left the house, with only a bottle of milk and a piece of ham and a hunk of bread. The little sister, who was very wise for her years, said to the brother, "Our stepmother is not sending us to her granny, but to a wicked witch. We must be polite and kind to everyone, and never touch a crumb belonging to anyone else. Then, who knows, someone might help us." And they set off into the great gloomy wood.

Eventually, the children saw in the thickest of the trees a little hut. Nervously they peeped inside—and there lay the witch, with her head on the threshold, a foot in each corner, and her knees cocked up, almost touching the ceiling. "Who's there?" she snarled.

Though the twins were terrified, they answered politely. "Good morning, Granny. Our stepmother has sent us to serve you."

"See that you do it well, then," growled the witch. "If I am pleased with you, I'll reward you, but if I am not, I'll cook you in the oven!"

So saying, she set the girl down to spin yarn, and she gave the boy a sieve in which to carry water from the well, and she herself went out into the wood.

The girl began weeping bitterly because she could not spin. But suddenly she heard hundreds of little feet, and from every hole in the hut mice came pattering, squeaking and saying:

"Little girl, why are your eyes so red?

If you want help, then give us some bread."

And the girl gave them some of her bread. Then the mice told her that the witch had a cat, and the cat was very fond of ham. If she would give the cat her ham, it would show her the way out of the wood, and in the meantime they would spin the yarn for her. So the girl set out to look for the cat, and, as she was hunting about, she met her brother. He was in great trouble because he could not carry water from the well in a sieve, as it came pouring out as fast as he put it in.

As she was trying to comfort him they heard a rustling of wings, and a flight of wrens alighted on the ground beside them. The wrens said:

"Give us some crumbs, then you need not grieve.

For you'll find that water will stay in the sieve."

Then the twins crumbled some of their bread on the ground, and the wrens pecked it and chirped. When they had eaten the last crumb they told the boy to fill up the holes of the sieve with clay, and then to draw water from the well. So he did what they said, and carried the sieve full of water into the hut without spilling a drop.

When they entered the hut the cat was curled up on the floor. They stroked her, and fed her with ham, and said to her: "Cat, tell us how to get away from the witch."

The cat thanked them for the ham, and gave them

a pocket handkerchief and a comb, and told the children what they should do with them to escape. The cat had scarcely finished speaking when the witch returned.

"Well, you have done well enough for today," she grumbled, "but tomorrow you'll have something more difficult to do, and if you don't do it well, straight into the oven you go."

Half dead with fright, the poor children lay down to sleep on a heap of straw in the corner of the hut. They dared not close their eyes and scarcely breathed.

In the morning the witch gave the girl two pieces of linen to weave before night, and the boy a pile of wood to chop. Then the witch left them to their tasks and went out into the wood.

As soon as she was out of sight the children took the comb and the handkerchief and, holding hands, they ran, and ran, and ran. First they met the witch's watchdog, who was going to tear them to pieces, but they threw the remains of their bread to him, and he ate it and wagged his tail. Then they were hindered by the birch trees, whose branches almost poked their eyes out. But the little sister tied the twigs together with her hair ribbon, and they got past safely and came out onto the open fields.

In the meantime, in the hut, the cat was busy weaving the linen. The witch returned to see how the children were getting on, and she crept up to the window and whispered: "Are you weaving, my dear?"

"Yes, Granny, I am weaving," answered the cat.

Then the witch realized that the children had escaped! She was furious at the cat, and screeched, "Why did you let the children leave the hut?"

But the cat spat and answered, "I have served you all these years and you never even threw me a bone, but the children gave me their own piece of ham."

Then the witch was furious with the watchdog and with the birch trees, because they had let the children pass. But the dog answered , "I have served you all these years and you never gave me so much as a crust, but the children gave me their own loaf of bread."

And the birch rustled its leaves and said, "I have

served you longer than I can say, and you never even tied a bit of twine round my branches, but the children bound them up with their bright ribbon."

So the witch saw there was no help to be got from her old servants, and she mounted her broom and set off after the children herself. As the twins ran they heard the sound of the broom close behind them. They remembered what the cat had told them and threw the handkerchief over their shoulders. Instantly, a deep, broad river flowed behind them.

It took the witch a long time to find a place to ride over on her broomstick, but at last she got across, and continued the chase faster than before.

As the children ran they heard the broom close behind them, so, quick as a thought, they did what the cat had told them and threw the comb down on the ground. In an instant, a dense forest sprang up, in which the roots and branches were so closely intertwined, that it was impossible to force a way through it. When the witch came to it she found that there was nothing for it but to turn round and go

back to her hut, tearing her hair with rage.

The twins ran straight on till they reached home. They told their father all that they had suffered, and he was so angry with their stepmother that he drove her out of the house and never let her return. Then he and the children lived happily ever after.

Aladdin and the Wonderful Lamp

An extract from *The Arabian Nights Entertainments,*
retold by Andrew Lang

THERE ONCE LIVED a poor tailor, who had a son called Aladdin, a careless, idle boy who would do nothing but play all day long in the streets with little idle boys like himself. This so grieved the father that he died; yet, in spite of his mother's tears and prayers, Aladdin did not mend his ways. One day, when he was playing in the streets as usual, a stranger asked him his age and if he was the son of Mustapha the tailor.

"I am, sir," replied Aladdin, "but he died a long while ago."

On this the stranger, who was a famous African

magician, hugged him and kissed him, saying, "I am your uncle! I recognized you because you look so like my brother. You must go to your mother and tell her I am coming."

Aladdin ran home, and told his mother of his newly found uncle.

"Indeed, child," she said, "your father had a brother, but I always thought he was dead."

However, she prepared supper, and told Aladdin to get ready to welcome his uncle. The strange man came laden with gifts of wine and fruit. He kissed the place where Mustapha used to sit, bidding Aladdin's mother not to be surprised at not having seen him before, as he had been out of the country for forty years. He then turned to Aladdin and asked him his trade, at which the boy hung his head, while his mother burst into tears. On learning that Aladdin was idle and refused to learn a trade, he offered to rent a shop for him and stock it for him. The very next day he bought Aladdin a fine suit of clothes, and took him all over the city, showing him the sights. At nightfall, he brought Aladdin home to his mother, who was overjoyed to see her son so fine.

On the following day, he led Aladdin into some beautiful gardens a long way outside the city gates. They sat down by a fountain, and the magician pulled a cake from his girdle, which he divided between them. They then journeyed onward till they almost reached the mountains. Aladdin was so tired that he begged to go back, but the magician won him over with pleasant stories, and led him on.

At last they came to two mountains divided by a narrow valley.

"We will go no farther," said the false uncle. "I will show you something wonderful; you gather up sticks while I kindle a fire."

When it was lit the magician threw a powder on it, at the same time saying some magical words. The earth trembled a little and opened in front of them to show a square, flat stone with a brass ring in the middle to raise it by. Aladdin tried to run away, but the magician caught him and gave him a blow that knocked him down.

"What have I done, uncle?" Aladdin begged.

The magician replied, more kindly, "Fear nothing, but obey me. Beneath this stone lies a treasure which is to be yours, and no one else may touch it, so you must do exactly as I tell you."

At the word 'treasure', Aladdin forgot his fears, and grasped the ring as he was told, saying the names of his father and grandfather. The stone came up quite easily and some steps appeared.

"Go down," said the magician; "at the foot of those steps you will find an open door leading into three large halls. Tuck up your gown and go through them without touching anything, or you will die instantly. These halls lead into a garden of fine fruit trees. Walk on till you come to an alcove in a terrace where stands a lighted lamp. Pour out the oil it contains and bring the lamp to me."

The magician drew a ring from his finger and gave it to Aladdin, wishing him good luck.

Nervously, Aladdin crept down the stairs. He found everything as the magician had said. He gathered some fruit off the trees, got the lamp, and hurried back to the mouth of the cave.

The magician cried out, "Make haste and give me the lamp."

But Aladdin was suspicious. "Only when I'm safely out of the cave," he yelled back.

The magician flew into a terrible rage. Throwing some more powder on the fire, he said more magic words, and the stone rolled back into its place.

The magician left Persia forever, which plainly showed that he was no uncle of Aladdin's. He was a cunning magician who had read in his magic books of a wonderful lamp, which would make him the most powerful man in the world. Though he alone knew where to find it, he could only receive it from the hand of another. He had picked out the foolish Aladdin for this purpose, intending to get the lamp and kill him afterward.

For two days Aladdin remained in the dark, crying and wailing. At last he clasped his hands in prayer, and in doing so rubbed the ring, which the magician had forgotten to take from him. Immediately an enormous and frightful genie rose out of it, saying, "What do you want from me? I am the Slave of the Ring, and will obey you in all things."

Aladdin fearlessly replied, "Deliver me from this place!" whereupon the earth opened, and he found himself outside. As soon as his eyes could bear the light he went home, where he fainted from exhaustion and shock the minute he went through the door. When he came to, he told his mother what had happened, and showed her the lamp and the fruits he had gathered in the garden, which were in reality precious stones. He then asked for some food.

"Alas, child!" she said. "Our cupboards are bare. But I have spun a little cotton and will go and sell it."

"No," Aladdin protested. "You keep the cotton. I'll go and sell this rusty old lamp instead."

The lamp was indeed very dirty, and Aladdin's mother began to rub it to clean it, so that it might fetch a higher price. Instantly a hideous genie appeared, and asked what she wanted. She fainted, but Aladdin, snatching the lamp, said boldly, "Fetch us something to eat!"

The genie returned with a silver bowl, twelve silver plates containing rich meats, two silver cups, and two bottles of wine.

Aladdin's mother came to and couldn't believe her eyes. "Wherever did all this come from?" she said.

"Don't ask, just eat," Aladdin replied, grinning.

So they sat and tucked in, and Aladdin told his mother about the lamp. She begged him to sell it, and have nothing to do with devils.

"No," said Aladdin, "luck has brought it to me, so we will use it—and the ring too."

When they had eaten everything the genie had brought, Aladdin sold the silver plates. He then summoned the genie, who gave him another set of plates—and thus they lived for many years.

How Bradamante Conquered the Wizard

From Andrew Lang's *Red Romance Book*

F ROM CHILDHOOD, Bradamante had loved play-fighting with swords and bows and arrows, and her main joy was to mount the most fiery horses in her father's stable. So as well as growing up beautiful, she became tall and strong. She liked to put on men's armor and take part in tournaments among the most valiant knights. In fact, it was rare that she failed to carry off the prize.

Of course so wise and beautiful a maiden had no lack of wooers, but Bradamante wasn't interested in any of them—except the brave Sir Roger. But she kept her love secret and was content to wait till Roger thought fit to claim her as his bride.

One day, Bradamante heard the news that Roger had disappeared, and no one knew where. She didn't weep nor wail nor even utter a word, but the next morning she sharpened her sword and fastened her helmet and rode off to seek him.

Through many adventures, she pushed on till she crossed a mountain, and reached a valley watered by a stream and shaded by trees. There on the bank lay a young man with his head buried in his hands and seemingly in deepest misery. He told Bradamante that he had been out riding with a damsel whom he had lately freed from the power of a dragon. He had hoped to marry the lady, but as they rode along, a winged horse guided by a man in black swooped down and snatched her away.

"Since that day," he explained, "I have sought her through forests and over mountains, wherever I heard that a wizard's den was to be found. But each time it was a false hope that lured me on. Now, I am sure that my beloved is held captive among the rocky slopes nearby—but I am at a loss how to rescue her."

"If it is there she lies, I will free her," cried Bradamante; but the knight shook his head.

"I have visited that dark and dreadful place," he said. "It is like the valley of death. Among black and pathless precipices stands a rock, and on its top is a castle whose walls are of steel. It was built, so I have since learned, by a magician, and none can capture it. I have watched two knights try and fail—one was Gradasso, King of Sericane, and the other (and the more valiant) was the noble young Sir Roger."

Bradamante's heart leaped at the mention of Roger, but she only said, "What happened to them?"

"I told them my sad tale, and they answered in knightly fashion that they would fight for the freedom of my lady. The king tried to attack the castle first, but in an instant there shot into the sky the winged horse bearing his master, clad as before in black armor. He darted down, and thrust a spear into Gradasso's side. Roger ran to help, never thinking of what might befall himself. But, in truth, how could mortal men fight with a wizard who had studied all the magic of the East, and had a winged horse to help him? His movements were so swift that they couldn't see where to strike him, and soon both Gradasso and Roger were covered with wounds, while their enemy had never once been touched.

"Their strength as well as their courage began to fail against this strange warfare. Then the wizard drew a silken covering from off his shield and held the shield toward them as a mirror. It blazed so bright that I had to cover my eyes, and when I opened them again, I was alone upon the mountain. Roger and Gradasso had doubtless been carried by the wizard to the dark cells of the prison, where my fair lady also lies," answered the knight, and he again dropped his head upon his hands.

Now this knight was a wicked man called Count Pinabello, but Bradamante did not know that she shouldn't trust him.

"Please, take me to the castle," she cried, thinking joyfully that her quest to find Roger was at an end.

"I will lead you there, if
you so desire to meet certain doom,"
answered the knight, with an evil glint in his eye.

So they set forth, but Pinabello did not lead
Bradamante to the castle. Instead, he led her to the
mouth of a dark, steep cavern—and then he pushed
her down!

Bradamante tumbled to the very bottom and lay there for a while, bruised and shaken. When she became used to the darkness, she stood up and looked around. 'There may be some way out,' she thought, noting that the cave was less gloomy than she had fancied, and felt round the walls. On one side there seemed to be a passage, and going cautiously down it she found that it ended in a sort of church, with a lamp hanging over the altar.

At this moment there opened a little gate, and through it came a lady. She was bare-footed, with streaming hair.

"Oh Bradamante," she said, "I have waited a long time for you. Here lies the tomb of the great magician Merlin. Before he died, he prophesied that one day you would find your way here. He commanded me to come here from a far-distant land and help you."

At that, a voice rose up from the tomb nearby, where Merlin had laid buried for many hundreds of years. "It is foretold that you will be the wife of

Roger," it boomed. "So take courage and follow the path that leads you to him. Let nothing turn you aside until you have overthrown the wizard who holds him captive."

Then the voice ceased, and the lady explained that she was Melissa, a kind sorceress who went through the world seeking to set wrongs right. She showed Bradamante a book that foretold all the glories that Bradamante and Roger's children would achieve.

"Tomorrow at dawn," she said when she had finished and put away the magic scroll, "I myself will lead you to the wizard's castle."

Next morning Melissa and Bradamante rode out from the cavern by a secret way. They passed over rushing rivers, and climbed high precipices, and as they went Melissa taught Bradamante how to try to set Roger free.

"No man, however brave, could withstand the wizard, who has his magic mirror as well as his flying horse to aid him. If you would reach Roger, you must first get possession of a ring owned by a man called

Brunello, who is riding only a few miles in front of us. In the presence of this ring all charms and sorceries lose their power; but, take heed, for to outwit Brunello is no easy task."

"It is good fortune indeed that Brunello should be so near us," answered Bradamante joyfully. "But how shall I obtain his ring?"

"You must fall to talking with him upon magic and enchantments," replied Melissa, "but beware lest he guess who you are or what your business. Lead him on till he offers himself to be your guide to the wizard's castle. As you go, strike him dead, before he has time to spy into your heart, and, above all, before he can slip the ring into his mouth. If he does that, you lose Roger forever."

Having said all this Melissa bade Bradamante farewell, and they parted with tears and promises of meeting again speedily. Bradamante entered an inn close by, where Brunello was already seated. She knew who he was straight away—but he knew her too, for many a time he had seen her at jousts and tournaments. Both pretending not to know each other, they fell into talk, and discussed the castle and the knights who lay imprisoned inside.

"I have dared to try many perilous adventures," said Bradamante at length, "and I have never failed to trample my foes underfoot. If only I had a guide to take me to the castle, I myself would challenge this wizard to deadly combat."

Brunello offered his own services and together they climbed the mountain till they stood at the foot of the castle. "Look at those walls of steel that crown the precipice," began Brunello; but before he could say more a strong girdle was passed round his arms, which were fastened tightly to his side. In spite of his cries and struggles, Bradamante drew the ring off his finger and placed it on her own, though kill him she would not. Then she seized a horn that hung nearby from a cord and, blowing a loud blast, waited calmly for the magician to answer.

Out he came on his flying steed, bearing on his left arm his silken-covered shield, while he uttered spells

HORRIBLE HAGS AND WICKED WARLOCKS

that had laid low many a knight and lady. Bradamante heard them all, and was not any the worse for the most evil of them.

Furious at his defeat, the wizard snatched the cover from the shield, and Bradamante, knowing full well what was to follow, sank heavily on the ground. At this the wizard covered his shield once more, and guided his steed swiftly to where the maiden lay. After that, unclasping a chain from his body, he bent down to find her. It was then that she lifted her ringed hand, and saw that before her stood an old man with white hair and a face scarred with sorrow.

"Kill me, I pray you, gentle lady," cried the magician, "yet know before I die that it is only because I love Roger that I have caused so much misery to so many gallant knights and fair damsels. I am Atlantes, the servant whose job it was to watch over him in childhood and use my magical powers to keep him from harm. As Roger grew to manhood, he was always the bravest and best in deeds of chivalry. So reckless was he, that many a time it needed all my magic to bring him back to life when seemingly he lay dead. At length, to keep him from harm, I built this castle, and filled it with all that was beautiful, and, as you know, with knights and ladies to be his companions. When everything was ready I captured Roger himself. Now, take my horse and shield, and throw open wide the castle doors—do what you will, but leave me only Roger."

The heart of Bradamante was not usually deaf to the sorrows of others, but this time it seemed turned to stone.

"Your horse and shield I have won for myself," she said, "and haven't you learned that it is useless to war against fate? It is fate that has given you into my hands. Therefore, lead the way to the gate, and I will follow you."

They climbed in silence the long flight of steps leading to the castle; then Atlantes stooped and raised a stone on which was engraved strange and magic signs. Beneath the stone was a row of pots filled with undying flames, and on these the wizard let the stone fall. In a moment there was a sound as if all the rocks on the earth were split, the castle vanished into the air, and with it Atlantes.

Instead, a troop of knights and ladies stood before Bradamante, who saw and heard only Roger.

The Master and His Pupil

Based on the folk tale of the sorcerer's apprentice,
retold by Joseph Jacobs in *English Fairy Tales*

THERE WAS ONCE a very learned man in the north-country who knew all the languages under the sun, and who was acquainted with all the mysteries of creation. He had one big book bound in black leather and clasped with iron, and chained to a table that was made fast to the floor. When he read out of this book, he unlocked it with an iron key, and none but he read from it, for it contained all the secrets of the spirit world. It told how many angels there were in heaven, and how they marched in their ranks, and sang in their choirs, and what their names and jobs were. And it told of the demons, how many there were, and what their names and powers were, and how they might be summoned, and made to do people's bidding.

Now the master had a pupil who was but a foolish lad. He acted as a servant, and was never allowed to look into the black book, or hardly to enter the private room.

One day the master was out, and the lad, as curious as could be, hurried to the magical chamber. He gazed at his master's wondrous apparatus for changing copper into gold and lead into silver, and the mirror in which his master could see all that was passing in the world, and the shell that whispered to his master what people were saying at that very moment. But the lad realized he could do nothing with these things. "I don't know the right words to utter," he sighed. "They are locked up in the big black book."

He looked round and saw that the book was unfastened! The master had forgotten to lock it before he went out. The boy rushed to it and opened the volume. It was written with red-and-black ink, and much of it he could not understand. But he put his finger on a line and spelled it through.

At once the room was darkened, and the house trembled; a clap of thunder rolled through the passage and the old room, and there stood before him a horrible, horrible form, breathing fire, and with eyes like burning lamps. It was the demon Beelzebub, whom he had called up to serve him.

"Set me a task!" bellowed Beelzebub, with a voice like the roaring of an iron furnace.

The boy only trembled, and his hair stood up.

"Set me a task, or I shall strangle thee!"

But the lad could not speak.

Then the evil spirit stepped toward him, and putting forth his hands, touched his throat. The fingers burned his flesh. "Set me a task!"

"Water that flower over there," cried the boy in despair, pointing to a geranium that stood in a pot on the floor.

Instantly the spirit left the room, but in another instant he returned with a barrel on his back, and poured its contents over the flower; and again and again he went and came, and poured more and more water, till it was ankle-deep on the floor of the room.

"Enough, enough!" gasped the lad, but the demon heeded him not; the lad didn't know the words by which to send him away, and still he fetched water.

It rose to the boy's knees and still more water was poured. It mounted to his waist, and Beelzebub still kept on bringing barrels full. It rose to his armpits, and he scrambled to the table-top. And now the water in the room stood up to the window and washed against the glass, and swirled around his feet on the table. It still rose; it reached his breast. In vain he cried; the evil spirit would not be dismissed, and to this day he would have been pouring water, and would have drowned all the world. But the master remembered on his journey that he had not locked his book, and therefore returned. At the moment when the water was bubbling about the pupil's chin, he rushed into the room and spoke the words that cast Beelzebub back into his fiery home.

The Little Mermaid

An extract from the tale by Hans Christian Andersen

THE LITTLE MERMAID went out from her garden, and took the road to the foaming whirlpools, behind which the sorceress lived. She had never been that way before. Neither flowers nor grass grew there, nothing but bare, gray, sandy ground stretched out to the whirlpool, where the water, like foaming mill-wheels, whirled round everything that it seized, and cast it into the fathomless deep. Through the midst of these crushing whirlpools the little mermaid was obliged to pass, to reach the dominions of the sea witch. And also for a long distance the only road lay right across a quantity of warm, bubbling mire, called by the witch her turfmoor. Beyond this stood her house, in the center of a strange forest, in which all the trees and flowers were polypi, half animals and half plants, they looked like serpents with a hundred heads growing out of the ground. The branches were long slimy arms, with fingers like flexible worms, moving limb after limb from the root to the top. All that could be reached in the sea they seized, and held fast, so that it never escaped from their clutches.

The little mermaid was so alarmed at what she saw, that she stood still, and her heart beat with fear, and she was very nearly turning back. But she thought of the prince, and of the human soul for which she longed, and her courage returned. She fastened her long, flowing hair round her head, so that the polypi might not seize hold of it. Then she darted forward as a fish shoots through the water, between the supple arms and fingers of the ugly polypi, which were stretched out on each side of her. She saw that each held in its grasp something it had seized with its numerous little arms, as if they were iron bands. The white skeletons of human beings who had perished at sea, and had sunk down into the deep waters, skeletons of land animals, oars, rudders, and chests of ships were lying tightly grasped by their clinging arms, even a little mermaid, whom they had caught and strangled, and this seemed the most shocking of all to the little princess.

She now came to a space of marshy ground in the wood, where large, fat water-snakes were rolling in the mire, and showing their ugly, drab-colored bodies. In the midst of this spot stood a house, built with the bones of shipwrecked human beings. There sat the sea witch, allowing a toad to eat from her mouth. She called the ugly water-snakes her little chickens, and allowed them to crawl all over her.

"I know what you want," said the sea witch, "it is very stupid of you, but you shall have your way, and it will bring you to sorrow, my pretty princess. You want to get rid of your fish's tail, and to have two supports instead of it, like human beings on earth, so that the young prince may fall in love with you, and that you may have an immortal soul." And then the witch laughed so loud and disgustingly, that the toad and the snakes fell to the ground, and lay there wriggling about. "You are just in time," said the witch, "for after sunrise tomorrow I should not be able to help you till the end of another year. I will prepare a magic potion for you, with which you must swim to land tomorrow before sunrise, and sit down on the shore and drink it. Your tail will then disappear, and shrink up into what mankind calls legs, and you will feel great pain, as if a sword were passing through you. But all who see you will say that you are the prettiest little human being they ever saw. You will still have the same floating gracefulness of movement, and no dancer will ever tread so lightly. But at every step you take it will feel as if you were treading upon sharp knives, and that the blood must flow. If you will bear all this, I will help you."

"Yes, I will," said the princess in a trembling voice, as she thought of the prince and the immortal soul.

"But think again," said the witch, "for once your shape has become like a human being, you can no more be a mermaid. You will never return through the water to your sisters, or to your father's palace again. And if you do not win the love of the prince, so that he is willing to forget his father and mother for your sake, and to love you with his whole soul, and allow the priest to join your hands that you may be man and wife, then you will never have an immortal soul. The first morning after he marries another your heart will break, and you will become foam on the crest of the waves."

"I will do it," said the little mermaid, and she became pale as death.

"But I must be paid also," said the witch, "and it is not a trifle that I ask. You have the sweetest voice of any who dwell here in the depths of the sea, and you believe that you will be able to charm the prince with it also, but this voice you must give to me; the best thing you possess will I have for the price of my draught. My own blood must be mixed with it, that it may be as sharp as a two-edged sword."

"But if you take away my voice," said the little mermaid, "what is left for me?"

"Your beautiful form, your graceful

walk, and your expressive eyes. Surely with these you can enchain a man's heart? Well, have you lost your courage? Put out your little tongue that I may cut it off as my payment, and then you shall have the powerful draught."

"It shall be," said the little mermaid.

Then the witch placed her cauldron on the fire to prepare the magic potion.

"Cleanliness is a good thing," said she, scouring the vessel with snakes, which she had tied together in a large knot. Then she pricked herself in the breast, and let the black blood drop into it. The steam that rose formed itself into such horrible shapes that no one could look at them without fear. Every moment the witch threw something else into the vessel, and when it began to boil, the sound was like the weeping of a crocodile. When at last the magic potion was ready, it looked like the clearest water. "There it is for you," said the witch. Then she cut off the mermaid's tongue, so that she became dumb, and would never again speak or sing.

"If the polypi should seize hold of you as you return through the wood," said the witch, "throw over them a few drops of the potion, and their fingers will be torn into a thousand pieces." But the little mermaid had no occasion to do this, for the polypi sprang back in terror when they caught sight of the glittering potion that shone in her hand like a twinkling star.

So she passed quickly through the wood and the marsh, and between the rushing whirlpools. She saw that in her father's palace the torches in the ballroom were extinguished, and all within asleep. But she did not venture to go in to them, for now she was dumb and going to leave them forever, she felt as if her heart would break. She stole into the garden, took a flower from the flowerbeds of each of her sisters, kissed her hand a thousand times toward the palace, and then rose up through the dark blue waters.

The Wicked Witch of the West

Adapted from *The Wonderful Wizard of Oz,*
by L Frank Baum

Dorothy lives in a farmhouse in Kansas, which is one day whisked into the air by a tornado—with her and her little dog Toto inside. It drops down into the Land of Oz, where Dorothy meets the Good Witch of the North, who gives her some silver shoes and tells her that to return home, she must go to the Emerald City and ask the Wizard of Oz for help. Dorothy travels down the Yellow Brick Road, befriending the Scarecrow, the Tin Woodman, and the Cowardly Lion. They go with her, as the Scarecrow wants to ask the Wizard for a brain, the Tin Woodman for a heart, and the Cowardly Lion for some courage. When they finally reach the Wizard, he agrees to help them—but only if they can kill the Wicked Witch of the West, who rules over the Winkie Country...

THE SOLDIER with the green whiskers led them to the gate out of the Emerald City.

"Which road leads to the Wicked Witch of the West?" asked Dorothy.

"There is no road," answered the Guardian of the Gates. "No one ever wishes to go that way."

"How, then, are we to find her?" enquired the girl.

"That will be easy," replied the Guardian of the Gates, "walk to the West, and when she knows you are in the country of the Winkies, she will find you and make you all her slaves."

"Perhaps not," said the Scarecrow, "for we mean to destroy her."

So they turned toward the West, walking over fields of soft grass dotted here and there with daisies and buttercups. The Emerald City was soon left far behind. And as they advanced the ground became rougher and hillier, for there were no farms nor houses in this country of the West, and the ground was untilled.

In the afternoon the sun shone hot in their faces,

for there were no trees to offer them shade, so that before night Dorothy and Toto and the Lion were tired, and lay down upon the grass and fell asleep, with the Woodman and the Scarecrow keeping watch.

Now the Wicked Witch of the West had but one eye, yet that was as powerful as a telescope, and could see everywhere. So, as she sat in the door of her castle, she happened to look around and saw Dorothy lying asleep, with her friends all about her. They were a long distance off, but the Wicked Witch was angry to find them in her country. So she blew upon a silver whistle that hung around her neck.

At once there came running to her from all directions a pack of great wolves. They had long legs and fierce eyes and sharp teeth.

"Go to those people," said the Witch, "and tear them to pieces."

"Are you not going to make them your slaves?" asked the leader of the wolves.

"No," the Witch answered, "one is of tin, and one of straw, one is a girl and another a lion. None of them is fit to work, so you may tear them all into small pieces."

"Very well," said the wolf, and he dashed away at full speed, followed by the others.

It was lucky the Scarecrow and the Woodman were wide awake and heard the wolves coming.

"This is my fight," said the Woodman, "so get behind me and I will meet them as they come."

He seized his ax, which he had made very sharp, and as the leader of the wolves came on the Tin Woodman swung his arm and chopped the wolf's

head from its body, so that it immediately died. As soon as he could raise his ax another wolf came up, and he also fell under the sharp edge of the Tin Woodman's weapon. There were forty wolves, and forty times a wolf was killed, so that at last they all lay dead in a heap before the Woodman.

Then he put down his ax and sat beside the Scarecrow, who said, "It was a good fight, friend."

They waited until Dorothy awoke the next morning. The little girl was quite frightened when she saw the great pile of shaggy wolves, but the Tin Woodman told her all. She thanked him for saving them and sat down to breakfast, after which they started again upon their journey.

Now this same morning the Wicked Witch came to the door of her castle and looked out with her one eye that could see far off. She saw all her wolves lying dead, and the strangers still traveling through her country. This made her angrier than before, and she blew her silver whistle twice.

A great flock of wild crows came flying toward her,

enough to darken the sky.

And the Wicked Witch said to the King Crow, "Fly to the strangers, peck out their eyes and tear them to pieces."

The wild crows flew in one great flock toward Dorothy and her companions. When the little girl saw them coming she was afraid.

But the Scarecrow said, "This is my battle, so lie down beside me all of you and you will not be harmed."

So they all lay upon the ground

except the Scarecrow, and he stood up and stretched out his arms. And when the crows saw him they were frightened, as these birds always are by scarecrows, and did not dare to come any nearer. But the King Crow said, "It is only a stuffed man. I will peck his eyes out."

The King Crow flew at the Scarecrow, who caught it by the head and twisted its neck until it died. And then another crow flew at him, and the Scarecrow twisted its neck also. Soon there were forty crows, and forty times the Scarecrow twisted a neck, until at last all were lying dead beside him. Then he called to his companions to rise, and again they started upon their journey.

When the Wicked Witch looked out again and saw all her crows lying in a heap, she got into a terrible rage, and blew three times upon her silver whistle.

Forthwith there was heard a great buzzing in the air, and a swarm of black bees came flying toward her.

"Go to the strangers and sting them to death!" commanded the Witch, and the bees turned and flew rapidly until they came to where Dorothy and her friends were walking. But the Woodman had seen them coming, and the Scarecrow had decided what to do.

"Take out my straw and scatter it over the little girl and the dog and the Lion," he said to the Woodman, "then the bees will not be able to sting them." This the Woodman did, and as Dorothy lay close beside the Lion and held Toto in her arms, the straw covered them entirely.

The bees came and found no one but the Woodman to sting, so they flew at him and broke off all their stings against the tin, without hurting the Woodman at all. And as bees cannot live when their stings are broken, that was the end of the black bees, and they lay scattered thick about the Woodman, like little heaps of fine coal.

Then Dorothy and the Lion got up, and the girl helped the Tin Woodman put the straw back into the Scarecrow again, until he was as good as ever. So they started upon their journey once more.

The Wicked Witch was so angry when she saw her black bees in little heaps like fine coal that she stamped her foot and tore her hair and gnashed her teeth. And then she called a dozen of her slaves, who were the Winkies, and gave them sharp spears, telling them to go to the strangers and destroy them.

The Winkies were not a brave people, but they had to do as they were told. So they marched away until they came near to Dorothy. Then the Lion gave a great roar and sprang toward them, and the poor Winkies were so frightened that they ran back as fast as they could.

When they returned to the castle the Wicked Witch beat them well with a strap, and sent them back to their work, after which she sat down to think what she should do next. She could not understand how all her plans to destroy these strangers had failed, but she was a powerful witch, as well as a wicked one, and she soon made up her mind how to act.

There was, in her cupboard, a Golden Cap, with a circle of diamonds and rubies running round it. This Golden Cap had a charm. Whoever owned it could call three times upon the Winged Monkeys, who would obey any order they were given. But no person could command these strange creatures more than three times. Twice already the Wicked Witch had used the charm of the Cap. Once was when she had made the Winkies her slaves, and set herself to rule over their country. The Winged Monkeys had helped her do this. The second time was when she had fought against the Great Oz himself, and driven him out of the land of the West. The Winged Monkeys had also helped her in doing this. Only once more could she use this Golden Cap, for which reason she did not like to do so until all her other powers were exhausted. But now that her wolves and her crows and her bees were gone, and her slaves had been scared away by the Cowardly Lion, she saw there was only one way left to destroy Dorothy and her friends.

So the Wicked Witch took the Golden Cap and placed it on her head. Then she stood upon her left foot and said slowly: "Ep-pe, pep-pe, kak-ke!"

Next she stood upon her right foot and said: "Hil-lo, hol-lo, hel-lo!"

After this she stood upon both feet and cried in a loud voice: "Ziz-zy, zuz-zy, zik!"

The charm began to work. The sky darkened and a rumbling sound was heard. There was a rushing of wings, a chattering and laughing, and the sun came out to show the Wicked Witch surrounded by monkeys, each with a pair of wings on his shoulders.

One, the leader, and bigger than the others, flew down to the Witch and said, "You have called us for the third and last time. What do you command?"

"Go to the strangers who are within my land and destroy them all except the Lion," said the Wicked Witch. "Bring that beast to me, for I have a mind to harness him like a horse, and make him work."

"Your commands shall be obeyed," said the big monkey. Then, with a great deal of chattering and noise, the huge crowd of Winged Monkeys flew away to find the place where Dorothy and her three friends were walking.

Some of the monkeys seized the Tin Woodman and carried him through the air until they were over a country that was thickly covered with sharp rocks. Here they dropped the poor Woodman, who fell a great distance to the rocks, where he lay so battered and dented that he could neither move nor groan.

Some other monkeys caught the Scarecrow, and with their long fingers pulled all of the straw out of his clothes and head. They made his hat and boots and clothes into a small bundle and threw it into the top branches of a tall tree.

The remaining monkeys threw pieces of stout rope

around the Lion and wound many coils about his body and head and legs, until he was unable to bite or scratch or struggle in any way. Then they lifted him up and flew away with him to the Witch's castle, where he was placed in a small yard with a high iron fence around it, so that he could not escape.

But Dorothy they did not harm at all. She stood, with Toto in her arms, watching the awful fate of all her comrades and thinking it would soon be her turn. The leader of the Winged Monkeys flew up to her, his long, hairy arms stretched out and his ugly, cruel face grinning terribly. But then he saw the mark of the Good Witch's kiss upon Dorothy's forehead and stopped at once, motioning the other monkeys not to touch her.

"We cannot harm this little girl," he ordered them, "for look, she has the protection of the Power of Good, and that is far, far greater than the Power of Evil. The very most we can do is to transport her with care to the castle of the Wicked Witch and leave her there."

So, carefully and gently, they lifted Dorothy in their arms and carried her swiftly through the air until they came to the castle, where they set her down upon the front doorstep. Then the leader said to the Witch, "We have obeyed you as far as we were able. Your power over our band is now ended, and you will never see us again." Then all the Winged Monkeys, with much laughing and chattering and noise, flew into the air and were soon out of sight.

The Wicked Witch looked down at Dorothy's feet, and seeing the Silver Shoes, began to tremble with fear, for she knew what a powerful charm belonged to them. But then she looked into the child's eyes and saw that the little girl did not know of the wonderful power the Silver Shoes gave her. So the Wicked Witch laughed to herself, and said to Dorothy, very harshly and severely, "Come with me little girl, and see that you listen carefully to everything I tell you, for if you do not I will surely make an end of you, as I did of the Tin Woodman and the Scarecrow."

So Dorothy became a slave for the Wicked Witch, and realized that it would be harder than ever to get back to Kansas again.

The Horned Women

From Joseph Jacobs' *Celtic Fairy Tales*

A RICH WOMAN sat up late one night carding (combing) wool, while all the family and servants were asleep. Suddenly there came a knock at the door and a voice outside called, "Open! Open!"

"Who is there?" said the woman of the house.

"I am the Witch of one Horn," came the answer.

The mistress opened the door and a woman with a horn growing on her forehead entered, holding a pair of wool-carders. She sat down by the fire in silence, and began to card the wool with violent haste. Suddenly she paused, and said aloud, "Where are the women? They delay too long."

Then a second knock came to the door, and a voice called, "Open! Open!"

The mistress felt herself obliged to rise and open the door, and immediately a second witch entered, having two horns on her forehead, and in her hand a wheel for spinning wool.

"Give me a place," she said. "I am the Witch of two Horns," and she began to spin as quick as lightning. And so the knocks went on, and the call was heard, and the witches entered, until at last twelve women sat round the fire—the first with one horn, the last with twelve horns. And they carded the wool, and turned their spinning-wheels, and wound and wove, all singing together an ancient rhyme, but they didn't speak a word to the mistress of the house. Strange to hear and frightful to look upon were these twelve women, with their horns and their wheels. The mistress was frightened to death and tried to get up to call for help, but she could not move, nor could she utter a word or a cry, for the spell of the witches was upon her.

Then one of them called to her, "Rise and make us a cake."

Then the mistress searched for a jug to bring water from the well that she might make the cake mix, but she couldn't find one.

And the witches said to her, "Take a sieve and bring water in it."

So she took the sieve and went to the well; but the water poured through the holes, and she sat down by the well and wept.

Then a voice from the well said, "Take yellow clay and moss, and bind them together, and plaster the sieve so that it will hold."

This she did, and the sieve held the water.

Then the voice said again, "Go back to the house, and just before you enter, cry aloud three times, 'The mountain and the sky over it is all on fire'."

And she did so.

When the witches inside heard the call, a great and terrible cry broke from their lips, and they rushed forth with wild shrieks, and fled away back home.

Then the Spirit of the Well told the mistress of the house to enter and prepare her home against the enchantments of the witches if they returned again.

First, to break their spells, she sprinkled the water in which she had washed her child's feet, outside the door. Secondly, she took the cake which in her absence the witches had made of meal mixed with blood drawn from her sleeping family, and she broke the cake in bits, and placed a bit in the mouth of each sleeper, and they woke up, free from the witches' power. Lastly, she secured the door with a great crossbeam barred against it, so that the witches could not enter. Having done these things she waited.

The witches weren't long in coming back, and they raged and called for vengeance.

"Open! Open!" they screamed. "Open, feet-water!"

"I cannot," said the feet-water, "I am scattered on the ground, trickling away to the lake."

"Open, open, wood and trees and beam!" they cried to the door.

"I cannot," said the door, "for I am fixed and have no power to move."

"Open, open, cake that we have made and mingled with blood!" they cried again.

"I cannot," said the cake, "for I am completely broken and bruised."

Then the witches rushed through the air with great cries, and fled back home, uttering strange curses on the Spirit of the Well, who had wished their ruin. And the mistress and the house were left in peace.

Rapunzel

Retold by Andrew Lang in his *Red Fairy Book*,
after the Brothers Grimm

ONCE UPON A TIME there lived a man and his
wife who were very unhappy because they had
no children. These good people had a little window at
the back of their house, which looked into the most
lovely garden, full of beautiful flowers and vegetables.
But the garden was surrounded by a high wall, and no
one dared to enter it, for it belonged to a witch of
great power, who was feared by the whole world. One
day the woman stood at the window overlooking the
garden, and saw there a bed full of the finest
rampion: the leaves looked so fresh and green that she
longed to eat them. The desire grew day by day, and

just because she knew she couldn't possibly get any, she pined away and became quite pale and wretched. Then her husband grew alarmed and said, "What ails you, dear wife?"

"Oh," she answered, "if I don't get some rampion to eat out of the garden behind the house, I know I shall die."

The man, who loved her dearly, thought to himself, 'Rather than let my wife die I will fetch her some rampion, no matter the cost.' So at dusk he climbed over the wall into the witch's garden, and, hastily gathering a handful of rampion leaves, he returned with them to his wife. She made them into a salad, which tasted so good that her longing for the forbidden food was greater than ever. If she were to know any peace of mind, there was nothing for it but that her husband should climb over the garden wall again, and fetch her some more. So at dusk he went over the wall, but when he reached the other side he drew back in terror, for there, standing before him, was the old witch.

"How dare you," she shrieked, "climb into my garden and steal my rampion like a common thief? You shall suffer for your foolhardiness."

"Oh!" he implored. "Forgive me but I was desperate. My wife saw your rampion from her window and longs for some so badly that she will surely die if she does not have some."

Then the witch grew calmer and said, "If it's as you say, you may take as much rampion as you like, but on one condition only—that you give me the child your wife will shortly bring into the world."

The man in his terror agreed to everything she asked. So as soon as the child was born the witch appeared, and having given it the name of Rapunzel, which is the same as rampion, she carried it off.

Rapunzel was the most beautiful child under the sun. When she was twelve years old the witch shut her up in a tower, in the middle of a great wood. The tower had neither stairs nor doors, only a small window high up at the very top. When the old witch wanted to get in she stood underneath and called out,

"Rapunzel, Rapunzel,
Let down your golden hair,"
for Rapunzel had wonderful
long hair, and it was as fine as
spun gold. Whenever she
heard the witch's voice she
loosened her plaits, and let
her hair fall down out of the window
to the ground below, and the old witch
climbed up by it.

After they had lived like this for a
few years, it happened one day that a
prince was riding through the wood and
passed by the tower. As he drew near it
he heard someone singing so sweetly that
he stood still and listened. It was lonely
Rapunzel trying to while away the time
by letting her sweet voice ring out into
the wood. The prince longed to see the
owner of the voice, but he sought in
vain for a door in the tower. He rode

home, but he was so haunted by the song he had
heard that he returned every day to the wood and
listened. One day, when he was standing behind
a tree, he saw the old witch approach and
heard her call out,

"Rapunzel, Rapunzel,
Let down your golden hair,"
then Rapunzel let down her plaits,
and the witch climbed up by them.
"So that's the staircase, is it?" said
the prince. "Then I too will climb
it and try my luck."

So on the following day, at
dusk, he went to the foot of
the tower and cried,

"Rapunzel, Rapunzel,
Let down your golden hair,"
and as soon as she had let it
down the prince climbed
up by it.

At first Rapunzel was

terribly frightened when a man came in, but the prince spoke to her so kindly that very soon Rapunzel forgot her fear. When he asked her to marry him she consented at once. For, she thought, 'He is young and handsome, and I'll certainly be happier with him than with the old witch.' So she put her hand in his and said, "Yes, I will gladly go with you, only how am I to get down out of the tower? Every time you come to see me you must bring a skein of silk with you, and I will make a ladder of them, and when it is finished I will climb down by it, and you will take me away with you on your horse."

They arranged that till the ladder was ready, he was to come to her every evening, because the witch was with her during the day. The old witch, of course, knew nothing of what was going on, till one day Rapunzel, not thinking of what she was about, turned to her and said, "How is it, good mother, that you are so much harder to pull up than the young prince? He is always with me in a moment."

"Oh, you wicked child!" cried the witch. "I

thought I had hidden you safely from the whole world but you have deceived me."

In her wrath she seized Rapunzel's beautiful hair and a pair of scissors—snip snap, off it came, and the beautiful plaits lay on the ground. And, worse than this, she was so hard-hearted that she took Rapunzel to a desert place, and there left her to live in loneliness and misery.

That same evening, the witch fastened the plaits on to a hook in the window, and when the prince came and called out,

"Rapunzel, Rapunzel,
Let down your golden hair,"

she let them down, and the prince climbed up as usual. Instead of his beloved Rapunzel he found the old witch, who fixed her evil, glittering eyes on him, and cried mockingly, "Ah, ah! You thought to find your lady love, but Rapunzel is lost to you forever— you will never see her more."

The prince was beside himself with grief, and in his despair he jumped right down from the tower.

Though he escaped with his life, the thorns among which he fell pierced his eyes. Then he wandered, blind and miserable, through the wood, eating nothing but roots and berries, and weeping for the loss of his lovely bride. So he wandered about for some years, as wretched and unhappy as he could be,

and at last he came to the desert place where Rapunzel was living. Suddenly he heard a voice that seemed strangely familiar to him. He walked eagerly in the direction of the sound, and when he was quite close, Rapunzel recognized him and hugged him and wept. But two of her tears touched his eyes, and in a moment they became quite clear again, and he saw as well as he had ever done. Then he led her to his kingdom, where they were received and welcomed with great joy, and they lived happily ever after.

The Mandarin and the Butterfly

From *American Fairy Tales* by L Frank Baum

A MANDARIN ONCE LIVED in Kiang-ho who was so exceedingly cross and disagreeable that everyone hated him. He snarled and stormed at every person he met and was never known to laugh or be merry under any circumstances. He hated boys and girls especially, for they jeered and made fun of him.

When he had become so unpopular that no one would speak to him, the emperor heard about it and commanded him to emigrate to America. This suited the mandarin very well; but before he left China he stole the Great Book of Magic that belonged to the wise magician Haot-sai. Then, gathering up his little store of money, he took a ship for America. He settled in a city of the midwest and started a laundry.

One day, as the ugly one was ironing in the basement of his shop, he looked up and saw a crowd of childish faces pressed against the window. He tried to drive them away, but as soon as he returned to his work they were back at the window, mischievously smiling down upon him. The mandarin uttered horrid words in the Manchu language and made fierce gestures; but this did no good at all. The children stayed as long as they pleased, and they came again the very next day as soon as school was over, and likewise the next day, and the next. For they saw their presence at the window bothered the Chinaman and were delighted accordingly.

The following day being Sunday the children did not appear, but as the mandarin worked in his little shop, a big butterfly flew in at the open door and fluttered about the room.

The mandarin closed the door and chased the butterfly until he caught it. He pinned it against the wall by sticking two pins through its beautiful wings. This did not hurt the butterfly, there being no feeling in its wings, but it made it a safe prisoner. This butterfly was of large size and its wings were

exquisitely marked by gorgeous colors laid out in regular designs, just like the stained-glass windows of a cathedral.

The mandarin now opened his wooden chest and drew forth the Great Book of Magic he had stolen from Haot-sai. Turning the pages slowly he came to a passage describing how to understand the language of butterflies. This he read carefully and then mixed a magic formula in a tin cup and drank it down with a wry face. Immediately thereafter he spoke to the butterfly in its own language.

"You are my prisoner," said the mandarin. "If I please I can kill you, or leave you on the wall to starve to death. But if you promise to obey me for a time and carry out my instructions, I will give you a long and pleasant life by means of powerful magic."

"I promise," answered the butterfly, "for even as your slave I will get some enjoyment out of life, while should you kill me—that is the end of everything!"

"Then, listen! You know children, do you not?"

"Yes, I know them. They chase me, and try to catch me, as you have done," replied the butterfly.

"They mock me, and jeer at me through the window," continued the mandarin. "Therefore, they are your enemies and mine! But with your aid and the help of the magic book we shall have a fine revenge for their insults."

"I don't care much for revenge," said the butterfly. "They are but children, and it is natural they should wish to catch such a beautiful creature as I am."

"Nevertheless, I care! And you must obey me," retorted the mandarin, harshly. "I, at least, will have my revenge."

Then he stuck a drop of molasses upon the wall beside the butterfly's head and said, "Eat that, while I read my book and prepare my magic formula."

So the butterfly feasted upon the molasses and the mandarin studied his book, after which he began to mix a magic compound in the tin cup.

When the mixture was ready he released the butterfly from the wall and said to it, "I command you to dip your two front feet into this magic compound and then fly away until you meet a child. Fly close, whether it be a boy or a girl, and touch the child upon its forehead with your feet. Whosoever is thus touched, the book declares, will at once become a pig, and will remain such forever after. Then return to me and dip you legs afresh in the contents of this cup. So shall all my enemies, the children, become miserable swine, while no one will think of accusing me of the sorcery."

"Very well, since such is your command, I obey," said the butterfly. Then it dipped its front legs, which were the shortest of the six, into the contents of the tin cup, and flew out of the door and away over the houses to the edge of the town. There it alighted in a flower garden and soon forgot all about its mission to turn children into swine.

In going from flower to flower it soon brushed the magic compound from its legs, so that when the sun began to set and the butterfly finally remembered its master, the mandarin, it could not have injured a child had it tried.

But it did not intend to try.

'That horrid old Chinaman,' it thought, 'hates children and wishes to destroy them. But I rather like children myself and shall not harm them. Of course I must return to my master, for he is a magician, and would seek me out and kill me; but I can deceive him about this matter easily enough.'

When the butterfly flew in at the door of the

mandarin's laundry, the Chinaman asked, eagerly, "Well, did you meet a child?"

"I did," replied the butterfly. "It was a pretty, golden-haired girl—but now 'tis a grunting pig!"

"Good! Good!" cried the mandarin, dancing joyfully about the room. "You shall have molasses for your supper, and tomorrow you must change two children into pigs."

The butterfly did not reply, and it ate the molasses in silence.

Next morning, by the mandarin's command, the butterfly dipped its legs in the mixture and flew away in search of children.

When it came to the edge of the town it noticed a pig in a sty, and alighting upon the rail of the sty it looked down at the creature and thought, 'If I could change a child into a pig by touching it with the magic compound, what could I change a pig into?'

Being curious to determine this fine point in sorcery the butterfly fluttered down and touched its front feet to the pig's nose. Instantly the animal disappeared, and in its place was a shock-headed, dirty-looking boy, which sprang straight from the sty and ran down the road uttering loud whoops.

"That's funny," said the butterfly to itself. "The mandarin would be very angry with me if he knew of this, for I have liberated one more of the creatures that bother him."

Then it flew into a rose bush, where it remained comfortably until evening. At sundown it returned to its master.

"Have you changed two of them into pigs?" he asked, at once.

"I have," lied the butterfly.

"Good! Good!" screamed the mandarin, in an ecstasy of delight. "Change every child you meet into a pig!"

"Very well," answered the butterfly, quietly, and ate its supper of molasses.

Several days were passed by the butterfly in the same manner. It fluttered aimlessly about the flower gardens while the sun shone, and returned at night to the mandarin with false tales of turning children into swine. Sometimes it would be one child which was transformed, sometimes it would be two, and occasionally three; but the mandarin always greeted the butterfly's report with intense delight and gave him molasses for supper.

One evening, however, the butterfly thought it might be well to vary the report, so that the mandarin might not grow suspicious; and when its master asked what child had been changed into a pig that day the lying creature answered, "It was a Chinese boy."

This angered the mandarin, who was in an especially cross mood. He spitefully snapped at the butterfly with his finger, and nearly broke its beautiful wing; for he forgot that Chinese boys had once mocked him and only remembered his anger for American boys.

The butterfly became very indignant at this abuse from the mandarin. It refused to eat its molasses and sulked all evening, for it had grown to hate the mandarin as much as the mandarin hated children.

When morning came it was still trembling with indignation, but the mandarin cried out, "Make haste, miserable slave; for today you must change four children into pigs, to make up for yesterday."

The butterfly did not reply. His little black eyes were sparkling wickedly, and no sooner had he dipped his feet into the magic compound than he flew full in the mandarin's face, and touched him upon his ugly, flat forehead.

Soon after a gentleman came into the room for his laundry. The mandarin was not there, but running around the place was a repulsive, scrawny pig, which squealed most miserably.

The butterfly flew away to a brook and washed from its feet all traces of the magic compound. When night came it slept in a rose bush.

Hansel and Grettel

Retold by Andrew Lang in his *Blue Fairy Book*,
after the Brothers Grimm

ONCE UPON A TIME there dwelt on the outskirts of a large forest a poor woodcutter with his wife and two children; the boy was called Hansel and the girl, Grettel. He had always little to live on, and a time came when he couldn't even provide them with daily bread. One night, unable to sleep with worry, he sighed and said to the children's stepmother, "What's to become of us? How are we to live?"

"I'll tell you what, husband," answered the woman, "early tomorrow morning we'll take the children out into the thickest part of the wood and leave them."

"No, wife," said her husband, "how could I!"

"Then we must all four die of hunger," said she, and she nagged and moaned till he agreed.

The children had been awake with hunger and had heard everything. Grettel wept bitterly, but Hansel got up, slipped on his coat, opened the back door and stole out. The moon was shining and the white pebbles that lay in front of the house glittered like silver. Hansel filled his pocket with as many of them as he could. Then he went back and said to Grettel, "Be comforted, my dear little sister, and go to sleep. I have a way to escape."

At daybreak, the woman came and woke the children. "Get up, we're all going to fetch wood," she commanded. She gave them each a bit of bread and said, "There's something for your lunch—it's all you're getting." Then they all set out together.

After they had walked for a little, Hansel stood and looked back at the house, and this he repeated again and again. His father observed him, and said, "Hansel, what are you gazing at?"

"Oh Father," said Hansel, "I am looking back at

my white kitten, which is sitting on the roof, waving me farewell." However Hansel had not looked back at his kitten, but each time had dropped one of the white pebbles out of his pocket on to the path.

When they had reached the middle of the forest and collected brushwood for a fire the woman said, "Now sit down, children, and rest. We are going to cut wood, but when we've finished we'll come back and fetch you."

Hansel and Grettel sat down beside the fire, and at midday ate their little bits of bread. When they had waited for a long time their eyes closed and they fell fast asleep.

It was pitch dark when they awoke. Grettel began to cry, and said, "How are we ever going to get out of the wood?"

But Hansel comforted her, saying, "Only wait, Grettel, till the full moon is up."

Then, he took his sister by the hand and followed the pebbles, which shone like bright coins in the moonlight and showed them the path. They walked on through the night, and at daybreak reached their home again—to the stepmother's great annoyance and the father's huge relief.

Not long afterward, one night the children again overheard their stepmother force their father to agree to abandon them in the forest. Hansel got up and wanted to go out and pick up pebbles again, as he had done the first time; but the woman had barred the door, and he couldn't get out.

At early dawn the woman came and made the children get up. They received their bit of bread, but it was even smaller than before. On the way into the wood Hansel crumbled it in his pocket, and every few minutes he stood still and dropped a crumb on the ground. "Hansel, what are you stopping and looking about for?" said the father.

"I'm looking back at my little pigeon, which is sitting on the roof waving me farewell," answered Hansel. But Hansel was gradually throwing all his crumbs on the path.

The woman led the children still deeper into the forest. Then a big fire was lit again, and she said, "Just sit down there, children. We're going into the forest to cut down wood, and in the evening when we're finished we'll come back to fetch you."

At midday Grettel divided her bread with Hansel, for he had strewn his all along their path. Then they fell asleep and didn't awake till it was pitch dark and they were still all alone. Hansel comforted his sister, saying, "Only wait, Grettel, till the moon rises, then we shall see the breadcrumbs I scattered along the path; they will show us the way back to the house." When the moon appeared they got up, but they found no crumbs, for the birds had picked them all up. "Never mind," said Hansel to Grettel, "you'll see we'll find a way out." But all the same they did not. They wandered about the whole night, and the next day, but they could not find a path out of the wood. They were very hungry, too, for they had nothing to eat but a few berries they found.

On the third morning they got deeper and deeper into the wood, and now they felt that if help did not come to them soon they must perish. At midday they stumbled across a little house, and when they came quite near they saw that it was made of bread and roofed with cakes, while the windows were made of transparent sugar. Hansel stretched up his hand and broke off a little bit of the roof to see what it was like, and Grettel went to the window and began to nibble at it.

Suddenly the door opened, and an ancient dame

leaning on a staff hobbled out. Hansel and Grettel were terrified, but the old woman said, "Oh, ho! You dear children, come in and stay with me, no ill shall befall you." She took them both by the hand and let them into the house, and laid a most sumptuous dinner before them—milk and sugared pancakes, with apples and nuts. After they had finished, two beautiful little white beds were prepared for them, and when Hansel and Grettel lay down in them they felt as if they had got into heaven.

The old woman had appeared to be most friendly, but she was really an old witch who had only built the little bread house in order to lure the children in. For when anyone came into her power she killed, cooked, and ate him!

Early in the morning, before the children were awake, she rose up, and seized Hansel with her bony hand and carried him into a stable, and barred the door on him; he might scream as much as he liked, it did him no good. Then she went to Grettel, shook her awake and cried, "Get up, you lazy-bones, fetch water and cook something for your brother. When he's fat I'll eat him up." Grettel began to cry bitterly, but it was no use; she had to do what the wicked witch bade her.

So the best food was cooked for poor Hansel, but Grettel got nothing but crab shells. Every morning the old woman hobbled out to the stable and cried, "Hansel, put out your finger, that I may feel if you are getting fat." But Hansel always stretched out a bone, and the old dame, whose eyes were dim, couldn't see it. The witch always thought it was Hansel's finger and wondered why he fattened so slowly. When four weeks had passed and Hansel still remained thin, she lost patience and decided to wait no longer.

"Grettel," she called, "be quick and get some water. Hansel may be fat or thin, I'm going to kill him tomorrow and cook him."

Oh, how the poor little sister sobbed! Early in the morning she had to go out and hang up the kettle full of water and light the fire. "First we'll bake," said the old dame. "I've heated the oven already and kneaded the dough." She pushed Grettel out to the blazing oven. "Creep in," said the witch, "and see if it's hot enough, so that we can shove in the bread." For when she had got Grettel in she meant to close the oven and let the girl bake, that she might eat her up too.

But Grettel knew what she had in mind, and said, "I don't know how I'm to do it. How do I get in?"

"You silly goose!" said the hag. "The opening is big enough, see, I could get in myself," and she crawled toward it and poked her head into the oven. Then Grettel shoved her right in, shut the iron door, and drew the bolt. Gracious, how she yelled! It was quite horrible. But Grettel fled, and the wretched old woman was left to perish miserably.

Grettel flew straight to Hansel, opened the stable-door, and cried, "Hansel, we are free, the old witch is dead." Then Hansel sprang like a bird out of an opened cage. How they rejoiced, and jumped for joy, and kissed one another! They went back into the old hag's house, and here they found, in every corner of the room, boxes with pearls and precious stones, which they crammed into their clothes.

"Now," said Hansel, "let's get well away."

When they had wandered about for some hours, the wood became more and more familiar to them, and at length they saw their father's house in the distance. Then they set off to run and, bounding into the room, fell on their father with joy. He had been despairing since he left them in the wood, and the wicked stepmother had died. Grettel shook out her apron so that the pearls and precious stones rolled about the room, and Hansel threw down one handful after the other out of his pocket. Thus all their troubles were ended, and they lived happily ever after.

DARING DEEDS AND RECKLESS RESCUES

The Terrible Head

The tale of Perseus and the Gorgon,
retold by Andrew Lang from the *Blue Fairy Book*

ONCE UPON A TIME there was a king whose only
child was a girl. The king was told by a prophet
that his daughter's son should kill him. This news
terrified him so much that he decided never to let his
daughter be married, for he thought it was better to
have no grandson at all than to be killed by his
grandson. He therefore called his workmen and bade
them dig a deep, round hole and then he had a prison
of brass built in the hole. When it was finished, he
locked up his daughter. No man ever saw her, and she
only saw the sky and the sun, for there was a wide

open window in the roof of the house of brass. So the princess would sit, watching the clouds float across, and wondering whether she should ever get out of her prison.

Now one day it seemed to her that the sky opened above her, and a great shower of shining gold fell through the window in the roof and lay glittering in her room. Not very long after, the princess had a baby, a little boy, but when the king, her father, heard of it he was very angry and afraid, for now the child was born that should be his death. Yet, he had not the heart to kill the princess and her baby outright, but he had them put in a huge, brass-bound chest and thrust out to sea, that they might either be drowned or starved, or perhaps come to a country where they would be out of his way.

So the princess and the baby floated in the chest all day and night, eventually driven by the waves against the shore of an island. There it lay till a man of that country came past and saw it, and dragged it onto the beach. When he had broken it open—behold! There was a beautiful lady and a little boy. He took them home, and was very kind to them, and brought up the boy till he was a young man.

Now when the boy had come to his full strength the king of that country fell in love with his mother, and wanted to marry her, but he knew that she would never part from her boy. So he thought of a plan to get rid of the boy, and this was it: a great queen of a country not far off was going to be married, and this king said that all his subjects must bring him wedding presents to give her. He made a feast to which he invited them all, and they all brought expensive presents. But the boy had nothing, though he was the son of a princess, for his mother had nothing to give him. Then the rest of the company began to laugh at him, and the king said, "If you have nothing else to give, then you must go and fetch the Terrible Head."

The boy was proud, and spoke without thinking.

"Then I swear that I will bring the Terrible Head, if it may be brought by a living man. But of what head you speak I know not."

Then they told him that somewhere, a long way off, there dwelled three Dreadful Sisters, monstrous, ogrish women, with golden wings and claws of brass, and with serpents growing on their heads instead of hair. Now these women were so awful to look on that whoever saw them was turned at once into stone. And two of them could not be put to death, but the youngest, whose face was very beautiful, could be killed, and it was her head that the boy had promised to bring.

When he heard all this he was sorry that he had sworn to bring the Terrible Head, but he was determined to keep his oath. So he went out from the feast, and he went and sat down on a rock, looking toward the sea, and wondering how he should begin to fulfill his vow. Then he felt someone touch him on the shoulder. He turned and saw a young man like a king's son, having with him a tall and beautiful lady, whose blue eyes shone like stars. They were taller than mortal men, and the young man had a staff in his hand with golden wings on it, and two golden serpents twisted round it, and he had wings on his cap and on his shoes. The lady said that to kill the dreadful woman with the golden wings and the brass claws, and to cut off her head, he needed three things: first, a Cap of Darkness, which would make him invisible when he wore it; next, a Sword of Sharpness, which would cleave iron at one blow; and last, the Shoes of Swiftness, with which he might fly in the air.

Then the young man, taking off his own shoes, said, "These are the Shoes of Swiftness. You will use them till you have taken the Terrible Head, and then you must give them back to me. Now first you must go to the Three Gray Sisters, who live far off in the north, and are so cold that they have only one eye and one tooth among the three. You must seize the eye and refuse to give it up till they have told you the way to the Three Fairies of the Garden. They will give you the Cap of Darkness and the Sword of Sharpness, and show you how to wing beyond this world to the land of the Terrible Head. Now, go at once!"

The young man thanked them, fastened on the Shoes of Swiftness, and turned to say goodbye to the young man and the lady, but they had vanished. He leaped in the air to try the Shoes of Swiftness, and they carried him more swiftly than the wind to a place where the world ends, and all water is frozen, and there are no men, nor beasts, nor any green grass. In a blue cave in the ice he found the Three Gray Sisters, the oldest of living things. Their hair was as white as the snow, and their flesh of an icy blue, and they mumbled and nodded in a kind of dream, and their frozen breath hung around them like a cloud. The opening of the cave in the ice was narrow, and it was not easy to pass in without touching one of the Gray Sisters. But, floating on the Shoes of Swiftness, the young man managed to steal in, and waited till one sister said to another, who had the eye, "Sister, what do you see? Do you see old times coming back?"

"No, sister."

"Then give me the eye, for perhaps I can see farther than you."

Then the first sister passed the eye to the second, but as the second groped for it the boy caught it cleverly out of her hand, slipped from behind them out of the cold cave into the air, and laughed aloud.

When the Gray Sisters heard that they began to weep, for now they knew that a stranger had robbed them. They began to implore the boy to give them their eye back again, and he could not help being sorry for them, they were so pitiful. But he said he would never give them the eye till they told him the way to the Fairies of the Garden.

Then they wrung their hands miserably, but at last they told him how to reach the Island of the Fairies of the Garden. Then he gave them back the eye and at once flew away till he saw a beautiful island crowned with flowering trees. There he alighted, and there he found the Three Fairies of the Garden. They were like three very beautiful young women, dressed one in green, one in white, and one in red, and they were dancing and singing round an apple tree with apples of gold. These dancing fairies were very unlike the Gray Sisters, and they were glad to see the man, and treated him kindly. They gave him a wallet and a shield, and belted the Sword of Sharpness around his waist, and set the Cap of Darkness on his head, and told him that now even they could not see him though they were fairies. Then they each kissed him and wished him good fortune.

So the young man flew beyond the great river that lies coiled like a serpent round the whole world. And by the banks of that river, there he found the three Dreadful Sisters, all asleep beneath a poplar tree, with dead leaves all about them. Their golden wings were folded and their brass claws were crossed, and two of them slept with their hideous heads beneath their wings like birds, and the serpents in their hair writhed out from under the feathers of gold. But the youngest slept between her two sisters, and she lay on her back, with her beautiful face turned to the sky; and though she slept, her eyes were wide open.

If the boy had seen her he would have been changed into stone by the terror and the pity of it, she was so awful. But he had thought of a plan for killing her without looking on her face. As soon as he caught sight of the three from far off he took his shining shield from his shoulders, and held it up like

a mirror, so that he saw the Dreadful Sisters reflected in it, and did not see the Terrible Head itself. Then he came nearer and nearer, and drew the Sword of Sharpness and struck once, and the Terrible Head was cut from the shoulders of the creature, and the blood leaped out and struck him like a blow. But he thrust the Terrible Head into his wallet, and flew away without looking behind.

Then the two Dreadful Sisters who were left wakened, and rose in the air like great birds, and though they could not see him because of his Cap of Darkness, they flew after him up the wind, following by the scent through the clouds, like hounds hunting in a wood. They came so close that he could hear the clatter of their golden wings, and their shrieks to each other as they chased him. But the Shoes of Swiftness flew too fast for them, and at last their cries and the rattle of their wings died away as he crossed the great river that runs around the world.

Now the boy flew straight eastward, trying to seek his own country. But as he looked down from the air he saw a very strange sight—a beautiful girl chained to a stake at the high-water mark of the sea. The boy was very sorry for her and flew down and stood beside her. He took off the Cap of

The Terrible Head

Darkness and there he was, the handsomest young man she had ever seen in all her life—and he thought her the most beautiful girl in the world. With one blow of the Sword of Sharpness he cut the iron chain that bound her. She told him that she was the daughter of the king of that country, and that she had been tied there to be eaten by a monstrous beast out of the sea; for the beast came and devoured a girl every day and the lot had fallen on her. Now just as she was saying this the long, fierce head of a cruel sea creature rose out of the waves and snapped at the girl.

The boy whipped the Terrible Head out of his wallet and held it up. And when the sea beast leaped again its eyes fell on the head, and instantly it was turned into a stone.

Then the boy and the girl went to the palace of the king, her father, where everyone was weeping for her death, and they were married with the most splendid rejoicings. After a while, the boy and his bride set forth for his home. But whom should he meet in the streets but his own mother, flying for her life from the wicked king, who now wished to kill her because he found that she would never marry him! She was running for her life, and the wicked king was following her, brandishing a sword in his hand. Then the boy shouted out to the king, "I swore to bring you the Terrible Head, and see how I keep my oath!" The boy drew forth the head from his wallet, and when the king's eyes fell on it, he was immediately turned into stone, just as he stood there with his sword lifted!

Now the boy, his wife, and his mother traveled

back to the kingdom that was rightfully theirs and the wicked king died, so they were able to live long and happily after all their troubles.

Rushen Coatie

A Cinderella story,
from *More English Fairy Tales* by Joseph Jacobs

THERE WAS ONCE a king and a queen who had a pretty daughter. But the queen died, telling the girl on her deathbed, "My dear, after I am gone, there will come to you a little red calf, and whenever you want anything, speak to it, and it will give it you."

Now, after a while, the king married again—an ill-natured wife with three ugly daughters of her own, who hated the king's daughter. So they took all her fine clothes away from her, and gave her only a coat made of rushes. They called her Rushen Coatie, and made her sit in the kitchen nook, amid the ashes.

When dinnertime came, the nasty stepmother sent her out a thimbleful of broth, a grain of barley, a thread of meat, and a crumb of bread. But when she had eaten this, she was just as hungry as before, so she said to herself, "Oh, how I wish I had something to eat!"

Just then, what should come in but a little red calf, and it said to her, "Put your finger into my left ear." She did so, and found some nice bread. Then the calf told her to put her finger into its right ear, and she found there some cheese, and made a right good meal. And so it went on from day to day.

Now the king's wife thought Rushen Coatie would soon die from the little food she got, and she was surprised to see her as lively and healthy as ever. So she set one of her ugly daughters to watch at meal times. The daughter soon found out that the red calf gave food to Rushen Coatie, and told her mother. So her mother went to the king and told him she was longing to have some meat from a red calf. Then the king sent for his butcher, and had the little calf killed.

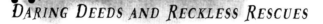

When Rushen Coatie heard of it, she sat down and
wept by its side, but the dead calf said:
    "Take me up, bone by bone,
       And put me beneath yon gray stone;
       When there is aught you want
       Tell it me, and that I'll grant."

So she did so, but could not find the shank bone of the calf.

Now the very next Sunday, all the folk were going to church in their best clothes, but the three ugly sisters told Rushen Coatie she must stay at home and make the dinner. When they all went to church, Rushen Coatie sat down and wept, but looking up, who should she see come limping in with a missing shank, but the dear red calf? And the red calf said to her, "Do not sit there weeping, but go, put on these clothes, and above all, put on this pair of glass slippers, and go on your way to church."

"But what will become of the dinner?" asked Rushen Coatie.

"Oh, do not worry about that," said the red calf.

So Rushen Coatie went off to church, and she was the grandest and finest lady there. Now there happened to be a young prince at the church, and he fell at once in love with her. But she came away before service was over, and was home before the others, and had taken off her fine clothes and put on her rushen coatie. She found the calf had covered the table, and the dinner was ready, and everything was in good order when the rest came home.

The three sisters said to Rushen Coatie, "Oh, if you had seen the fine lady in church today, that the young prince fell in love with!"

Then she said, "Oh! I wish you would let me go with you to the church next time."

But they said, "What should the likes of you do at church, you nasty thing? The kitchen nook is good enough for you."

So the next time they all went to church, Rushen Coatie was left behind to make dinner. But the red calf came to her again, gave her finer clothes than before, and she went to church. All the world was looking at her, and wondering where such a grand lady came from, and the prince fell more in love with her than ever before, and tried to find out where she went to. But she was too quick for him, and got home long before the rest, and the red calf had the dinner all ready.

The next Sunday the calf dressed her in even grander clothes than before, and she went to the church. The young prince was there again, and this time he put a guard at the door to keep her, but she took a hop and a run and jumped over their heads, and as she did so, down fell one of her glass slippers. She didn't wait to pick it up, but off she ran home, as fast as she could go, on with the rushen coatie, and the calf had all things ready.

The young prince put out a proclamation that whoever could put on the glass slipper should be his bride. All the ladies of his court went and tried to put on the slipper. They tried and tried, but it was too small for them all. Then he ordered one of his ambassadors to ride through the kingdom and find an owner for the glass shoe. He rode to town and castle, and made all the ladies try to put on the shoe. Many a one tried to get it on that she might be the prince's bride. But no, it wouldn't do, and many a one wept, because she couldn't get on the bonny glass shoe. The ambassador rode on and on till he came at

last to the house where there were the three
ugly sisters. The first two tried it and it
wouldn't do, and the queen, mad with
spite, hacked off the toes and heels
of the third sister. Then she could
put the slipper on, and the
prince was brought to
marry her, for he had
to keep his promise.
The ugly sister was
dressed all in her
best and was put
up behind the
prince on
horseback, and off
they rode in great
gallantry. But we all
know, pride must
have a fall, for as they
rode along a raven sang
out of a bush:

Rushen Coatie

"Hacked Heels and Pinched Toes
Behind the young prince rides,
But Pretty Feet and Little Feet
Behind the cauldron bides."

"What's that the bird sings?" said
the young prince.

"Nasty, lying thing," said the
stepsister, "never mind what it
is singing."

But the prince looked
down and saw her feet
dripping with blood, so
he rode back and put
her down. Then he
said, "There must be
someone that the
slipper has not been
tried on."

"Oh, no," said they,
"there's none but a dirty girl
who sits in the kitchen nook

and wears a rushen coatie."

The prince was determined to try the slipper on Rushen Coatie, but she ran away to the gray stone, where the red calf dressed her in her bravest dress. And then she went to the prince and the slipper jumped out of his pocket onto her foot, fitting her without any chipping or paring. So the prince married her that day, and they lived happy ever after.

The Dragon of the North

A myth from northern lands,
retold by Andrew Lang from the *Yellow Fairy Book*

VERY LONG AGO, there lived a terrible dragon who came out of the North and laid waste whole tracts of country, devouring both men and beasts. This dragon had a body like an ox, and legs like a frog, two short forelegs, and two long ones behind, and besides that it had a tail like a serpent. When it moved it jumped like a frog, and with every spring it covered half a mile of ground. Nothing could hunt it because its whole body was covered with scales, which were harder than stone or metal; its two great eyes shone by night, and even by day, like

the brightest lamps, and anyone who had the ill luck
to look into them became bewitched, and was obliged
to rush of his own accord into the dragon's jaws. In
this way the dragon was able to feed upon both men
and beasts without the least trouble to itself, as it
needed not to move from the spot where it was lying.
Its habit was to remain for several years in the same
place, and it would not move on till the whole
neighborhood was eaten up.

All the neighboring kings had offered rich rewards
to anyone who would be able to destroy the dragon,
either by force or enchantment, and many had tried
their luck, but all had failed miserably. However, there
was a saying that the dragon might be overcome by
one who possessed King Solomon's signet ring, upon
which a secret writing was engraved. This inscription
would enable anyone who was wise enough to
interpret it to find out how the dragon could be
destroyed. The problem was that no one knew where
the ring was hidden.

At last a young man, with a good heart and plenty

of courage, set out to search for the ring. He took his way toward the sunrise, because he knew that all the wisdom of old time comes from the East. After some years he met with a famous Eastern magician, and asked for his advice in the matter. The magician answered, "Mortal men have but little wisdom, and can give you no help. The birds of the air would be better guides to you if you could learn their language.

I can help you to understand it if you will stay with me a few days." The youth thankfully accepted the magician's offer. Each day for three days, he drank nine spoonfuls of a powerful potion, which made him able to understand the language of birds.

From then on, the youth never felt lonely as he walked along; he always had company, because he understood the language of birds; and in this way he learned many things that mere human knowledge could never have taught him. One afternoon, when he had sat down under a tree in a forest to eat his lunch, he heard two gaily plumaged birds discussing how he could only find King Solomon's lost ring if he sought help from the Witch maiden, who at dusk would wash her face in a magic spring to stay ever young and beautiful. The birds were going to watch, so the youth immediately resolved to follow the birds to the spring.

When the birds flew away, the young man's heart beat with anxiety lest he should lose sight of his guides, but by running as hard as he could he managed to keep them in view until they again

perched upon a tree. The young man ran after them until he was quite exhausted and out of breath, and after three short rests the birds at length reached a small, open space in the forest, on the edge of which they perched in a high tree. When the youth had overtaken them, he saw that there was a clear spring in the middle of the space. He hid himself at the foot of the tree and waited.

When the evening light had quite faded, and the full moon was shining down upon the forest, there came out of the wood a maiden, gliding over the grass so lightly that her feet seemed scarcely to touch the ground. The youth had never in his life seen a woman so beautiful. She went to the spring, looked up to the full moon, then knelt down and bathed her face nine times, then

looked up to the moon again and
walked nine times round the well,
singing. Then she dried her face
with her long hair, and was about
to go away, when her eye suddenly
fell upon the spot where the young
man was hiding. The youth knew he
had been discovered and rose, saying,
"Forgive me, beautiful maiden, if I
have offended by watching you."

The maiden answered kindly,
"Come and spend this night in my
house. You will sleep better on a
pillow than on damp moss."

The youth hesitated, but he heard the
birds saying from the top of the tree, "Go
where she calls you, but take care to give no
blood, or you will sell your soul." So the
youth went with her, and soon they reached a
beautiful garden, where stood a splendid house,
which glittered in the moonlight as if it was built

out of gold and silver. When the youth entered he found many splendid chambers, each one finer than the last. Hundreds of candles burned upon golden candlesticks, and shed a light like the brightest day. At length they reached a chamber where a table was spread with the most expensive dishes. At the table were placed two chairs, one of silver, the other of gold. The maiden seated herself upon the golden chair, and offered the silver one to her companion. They were served by maidens dressed in white, whose feet made no sound as they moved about, and not a word was spoken during the meal. Afterward the youth and the Witch maiden talked pleasantly together, until a woman, dressed in red, came in to remind them that it was bedtime. The youth was now shown into another room, containing a silken bed with down cushions, where he slept delightfully, yet he seemed to hear a voice near his bed which repeated to him, "Remember to give no blood!"

The next morning the maiden asked him whether he would not like to marry her and stay with her always in this wonderful place. The youth was tempted, but he remembered how the birds had called her a witch, and their warning always sounded in his ears. Therefore he answered cautiously and asked for some days to consider the matter. The maiden agreed, and to make the time pass pleasantly, she took the youth over every part of her beautiful dwelling, and showed him all her splendid treasures.

One day the maiden took him into a secret chamber, where a little gold box was standing on a silver table. Pointing to the box, she said, "Here is my greatest treasure, whose like is not to be found in the whole world. It is a precious gold ring. When you marry me, I will give you this ring as a marriage gift, and it will make you the happiest of mortal men. But in order that our love may last forever, you must give me for the ring three drops of blood from the little finger of your left hand."

When the youth heard these words a cold shudder ran over him, for he remembered that his soul was at stake. He was cunning enough, however, to conceal his feelings and to make no direct answer, but he only asked the maiden, as if carelessly, what was remarkable about the ring.

She answered, "No mortal is able entirely to understand the power of this ring, because no one thoroughly understands the secret signs engraved upon it. But even with my half-knowledge I can work great wonders. If I put the ring upon the little finger of my left hand, then I can fly like a bird through the air wherever I wish to go. If I put it on the fourth finger of my left hand I am invisible, and I can see everything that passes around me, though no one can see me. If I put the ring upon the middle finger of my left hand, then neither fire nor water nor any sharp weapon can hurt me. If I put it on the forefinger of my left hand, then I can produce whatever I wish. I can in a single moment build houses or anything I desire. Finally, as long as I wear the ring on the thumb of my left hand, that hand is so strong that it can break down rocks and walls. Besides these, the ring has other secret signs which, as

I said, no one can understand. No doubt it contains secrets of great importance. The ring formerly belonged to King Solomon, the wisest of kings, during whose reign the wisest men lived. But it is not known whether this ring was ever made by mortal hands, it is supposed that an angel gave it to wise King Solomon."

Then the youth had a cunning idea. "I do not think it possible that the ring can have all the power you say it has," he said. "Do let me try to see if I can do these wonderful things."

The maiden, suspecting no treachery, gave him the magic ring.

The youth asked her to remind him what finger he must put the ring on so that he could fly.

"Oh, the little finger of your left hand," the maiden answered, laughing.

The youth did so, and he soared into the air just like a bird.

When the maiden saw him flying away she thought he was playing, but the young man never came back.

Then the maiden saw she was deceived, and bitterly repented that she had ever trusted him with the ring.

The young man never halted in his flight until he reached the dwelling of the wise magician who had taught him the language of birds. The magician delightedly set to work at once to interpret the secret signs engraved upon the ring, but it took him seven weeks to make them out clearly. Then he told the youth he must have an iron horse cast, with little wheels under each foot, he must have huge iron chains and pegs made, and he must be armed with a spear as long and thick as a tree, which he would be able to wield by means of the magic ring upon his left thumb. And he told the youth how to use these to defeat the dragon.

The young man thanked the magician sincerely and quickly flew home through the air. After some weeks, he heard people say that the terrible Dragon of the North was not far off. The king announced publicly that he would give his daughter in marriage, as well as a large part of his kingdom, to whoever should free the country from the dragon. The youth went to the king and everything was prepared as he requested.

The young man rode out upon the iron horse to meet the dragon, pushing the spear against the ground, as if he were pushing off a boat from the land. The dragon had its monstrous jaws wide open! The youth trembled with horror and his blood ran cold, yet he did not lose his courage; but, holding the iron spear upright in his hand, he brought it down with all his might right through the dragon's lower jaw. Then quick as lightning he sprang from his horse before the dragon had time to shut its mouth. A fearful clap like thunder, which could be heard for miles around, now warned him that the dragon's jaws had closed upon the spear. When the youth turned round he saw the point of the spear sticking up high above the dragon's upper jaw, and knew that the other end must be fastened firmly to the ground; but the dragon had its teeth fixed in the iron horse, which was now useless. The youth now hastened to fasten down the chains to the ground by means of the

enormous iron pegs that he had provided. The death
struggle of the dragon lasted three days and three
nights; in its writhing it beat its tail so violently
against the ground, that at ten miles away the earth
trembled as if with an earthquake. When at length it
lost power to move its tail, the youth, with the help of
the ring, took up a stone that twenty ordinary men
could not have moved, and beat the dragon so hard
about the head with it that very soon the dragon lay
lifeless before him.

You can fancy how great was the rejoicing
when the news was spread abroad that the
terrible dragon was dead. His
conqueror was received into

the city with as much celebration as if he had been the mightiest of kings. The king's daughter was delighted to marry the hero, and a magnificent wedding was celebrated. But everyone forgot amid the general joy that they ought to have buried the dragon's monstrous body, for it began to have such a bad smell that the whole air was poisoned, which destroyed many hundreds of people.

In this distress, the king's son-in-law resolved to seek help once more from the Eastern magician, to whom he at once traveled through the air in the form of a bird. However, the Witch maiden had discovered by magic where the youth and her ring were. She changed herself into an eagle and watched in the air until the bird came in sight, then she pounced upon him and tore the ring from the ribbon he wore around his neck. Then the eagle flew down to the earth with her prey, and the two stood face to face once more in human form.

"Now, villain, you are in my power and you must pay!" cried the Witch maiden. She put the ring upon her left thumb, lifted the young man with one hand, and walked away with him to a deep cave. The maiden chained the young man's hands and feet to the rock so that he could not escape and declared, "Here you shall remain until you die. I will bring you enough food to prevent you dying of hunger, but you need never hope for freedom any more." And with these words she left him.

The old king and his daughter waited anxiously for many weeks for the prince's return, but no news of him arrived. They sent messengers far and wide to look for him. After searching for seven long years, they by good luck met with the old magician who had interpreted the signs on King Solomon's ring. The magician soon found out what they wished to know, and went himself to the cave where the unfortunate prince was chained up. The magician released him by the help of powerful magic, and took care of the prince until he became strong enough to travel. When he reached home he found that the old king had died, so that he was now raised to the throne. And now after his long suffering came prosperity, which lasted to the end of his life; but he never got back the magic ring, nor has it ever again been seen by mortal eyes.

The Demon with the Matted Hair

From *Indian Fairy Stories* by Joseph Jacobs

ONCE UPON A TIME, when Brahmadatta was King of Benares, his chief queen gave birth to a son who was actually a holy being called the Bodhisatta. On the baby's name day the king asked eight hundred wise men called Brahmans about his lucky marks. The Brahmans answered, "Full of goodness, great king, is your son, and when you die he will become king; he shall be famous and renowned for his skill with the five weapons, and shall be the chief man in all India." On hearing what the Brahmans had to say, the king and queen gave their son the name of the Prince of the Five Weapons: sword, spear, bow, club, and shield.

The boy grew up tall and strong, wise and good, and when he was sixteen years old, the king said to him, "My son, go and complete your education."

"Who shall be my teacher?" the lad asked.

"Go, my son; in the kingdom of Candahar, in the city of Takkasila, is a far-famed teacher from whom I wish you to learn. Take this, and give it to him for a fee." With that the king gave his son a thousand pieces of money and dismissed him.

The lad departed and was educated by this teacher, receiving the five weapons from him as a gift. When his studies were complete, the lad bade his teacher farewell, and began his journey back to Benares, armed with the five weapons.

On his way he came to a forest inhabited by the Demon with the Matted Hair. As he was entering the forest some men saw him, and cried out, "Hello, young sir, keep clear of that wood! There's a demon in it called he of the Matted Hair. He kills every man he sees!" And they tried to stop him. But the

Bodhisatta, having confidence in himself, went straight on, fearless as a maned lion.

When he reached the middle of the forest the demon showed himself. He made himself as tall as a palm tree; his head was the size of a pagoda, his eyes as big as saucers, and he had two tusks; he had the face of a hawk, a striped belly, and blue hands and feet. "Where are you going?" he shouted. "Stop! You'll make a meal for me!"

Said the Bodhisatta, "Demon, beware!" With this, he fitted to his bow an arrow dipped in deadly poison, and let it fly. The arrow stuck fast in the demon's hair. Then he shot and shot, till he had shot away fifty arrows; and they all stuck in the demon's hair. The demon snapped them all off short, and threw them down at his feet. Then he came up to the Bodhisatta, who drew his sword and struck the demon, threatening him all the while. His sword stuck in the demon's hair! The Bodhisatta struck him with his spear—that stuck too! He struck him with his club—and that stuck too!

"You, demon!" the Bodhisatta cried. "Did you never hear of me before—the Prince of the Five Weapons? This day will I pound you to powder!" And he hit at the demon with his right hand. It stuck fast in his hair! He hit him with his left hand—that stuck too! With his right foot he kicked him—that stuck too; then with his left—and that stuck too! Then he butted at the demon with his head, crying, "I'll grind you to dust!" And his head stuck fast like the rest.

Thus the Bodhisatta was five times snared, caught fast in five places. Yet he felt no fear and he was not even nervous.

The demon thought to himself, 'Here's a lion of a man! A noble man! Here he is, caught by a demon like me; yet he will not fear me a bit. Since I have ravaged this road, I never saw such a man.' He asked, "Why is it, young sir, that you are not at all frightened of me?"

"Why should I fear, demon?" the Bodhisatta replied. "In one life a man can die but once. Besides,

in my belly is a thunderbolt; if you eat me, you will never be able to digest it; this will tear your innards into tiny little bits and kill you, so you see we shall both perish. That is why I fear nothing." (The Bodhisatta meant the weapon of knowledge that he had within him.)

When he heard all of this the demon thought, 'This young man speaks the truth. A piece of the flesh of such a lionman as he would be too much for me to digest, if it were no bigger than a kidney bean. I will let him go!' So, being frightened to death, the demon let go of the Bodhisatta, saying, "Young sir, I will not eat you up. I set you free!"

And the Bodhisatta said, "Demon, I will go, as you say. You were born a demon, devourer of the flesh and gore of others, because you did wickedly in former lives. If you go on doing wickedly, you will go from darkness to darkness." Then he told the demon about the punishments that awaited evil creatures, and the rewards that awaited good beings. The demon vowed before the gods to change his ways.

Then the prince went on to Benares, armed with his five weapons, and became a king who ruled long and righteously.

Childe Rowland

From *English Fairy Tales* by Joseph Jacobs

CHILDE ROWLAND and his brothers twain
  Were playing at the ball,
And there was their sister, Burd Ellen,
in the midst, among them all.
Childe Rowland kicked it with his foot
And caught it with his knee;
At last as he plunged among them all
O'er the church he made it flee.
Burd Ellen round about the aisle
To seek the ball is gone,
But long they waited, and longer still,

And she came not back again.
They sought her east, they sought her west,
They sought her up and down,
And woe were the hearts of those brethren,
For she was not to be found.

So at last her eldest brother went to the Warlock Merlin and asked him if he knew where Burd Ellen was. "The fair Burd Ellen," said the Warlock Merlin, "must have been carried off by the fairies, because she went round the church 'widershins'—the opposite way to the sun. She is now in the Dark Tower of the King of Elfland; it would take the boldest knight in Christendom to bring her back."

"If it is possible," said her brother, "I'll do it, or perish in the attempt."

"Possible it is," said the Warlock Merlin, "but woe to he who attempts it, if he is not well taught beforehand what he is to do."

The eldest brother of Burd Ellen was not to be put off, so he begged the Warlock Merlin to tell him what to do, and then set out for Elfland.

But long they waited, and longer still,
With doubt and huge pain,
But woe were the hearts of his brethren,
For he came not back again.

Then the second brother got tired and sick of waiting, and he went to the Warlock Merlin and asked him the same as his brother. So he set out to find Burd Ellen.

But long they waited, and longer still,
With huge doubt and pain,
And woe were his mother's and brother's heart,
For he came not back again.

And when they had waited and waited a good long time, Childe Rowland, the youngest of Burd Ellen's brothers, wished to go, and begged his mother, the good queen, to let him go. She gave him his father's sword that never struck in vain and said the spell that would give it victory.

So Childe Rowland said goodbye and went to the cave of the Warlock Merlin. "Once more," he said to the Warlock, "tell how I may rescue Burd Ellen and her two brothers."

"Well, my son," said the Warlock Merlin, "there are but two things, simple they may seem, but hard they are to do. One thing to do, and one thing not to do. And the thing to do is this: after you have entered the land of Fairy, whoever speaks to you, till you meet the Burd Ellen, you must out with your father's sword and off with their head. And what you've not to do is this: bite no bit, and drink no drop, however hungry or thirsty you be; drink a drop, or bite a bit, while in Elfland you be and never will you see Middle Earth again."

So Childe Rowland thanked the Warlock Merlin and went on his way. He went along, and along, and still further along, till he came to the horse-herder of the King of Elfland feeding his horses. These he knew by their fiery eyes, and knew that he was at last in the land of Fairy. "Can you tell me," said Childe Rowland to the horse-herder, "where the King of Elfland's Dark Tower is?"

"I cannot tell you," said the horse-herder, "but go on a little further and you will come to the cow-herder, and he, maybe, can tell you."

Then, without a word more, Childe Rowland drew the good sword that never struck in vain, and off came the horse-herder's head. Childe Rowland went on, till he came to the cow-herder, and asked him the same question.

"I can't tell you," said he, "but go on a little farther, and you will come to the hen wife, and she is sure to know." Then Childe Rowland pulled out his good sword that never struck in vain, and off came the cow-herder's head. And he went on a little further, till he came to an old woman in a gray cloak, and he asked her if she knew where the Dark Tower of the King of Elfland was.

"Go on a little further," said the hen wife, "till you come to a round, green hill, surrounded with terrace-rings, from the bottom to the top; go round it three times, widershins, and each time say:

'Open, door! Open, door!

And let me come in,'

and the third time the door will open, and you may go in." Childe Rowland was just going on, when he remembered what he had to do; so he struck out with the good sword that never struck in vain, and off came the hen wife's head.

Then he went on, and on, and on, till he came to the round, green hill with terrace rings from top to bottom, and he went round it three times, widershins, saying each time:

"Open, door! Open, door!

And let me come in,"

and the third time the door did open, and he went in,

and it closed with a click. Childe Rowland was left in a kind of twilight, though there were neither windows nor candles, and he could not make out where the twilight came from. The walls and roof were made of a transparent rock, encrusted with bright stones. Childe Rowland went through this passage till at last he came to two wide and high folding doors that stood ajar. When he opened them, there he saw a glorious, large and spacious hall. The roof was supported by fine pillars, so large and lofty that the pillars of a cathedral were nothing compared to them. They were all of gold and silver, with wreaths of flowers composed of precious stones. Ornamented arches met in the middle of the roof, where hung by a golden chain an immense lamp made out of one big pearl. The hall was furnished in a manner equally grand, and at one end of it was a glorious couch of velvet, silk and gold, and there sat Burd Ellen, combing her golden hair with a silver comb. And when she saw Childe Rowland she stood up and said:

"God pity ye, poor luckless fool,
  What have ye here to do?
  Hear ye this, my youngest brother,
  Why didn't ye bide at home?
  Had you a hundred thousand lives
  Ye couldn't spare any a one.
  But sit ye down; but woe, O, woe,
  That ever ye were born,
  For come the King of Elfland in,
  Your fortune is forlorn."

Then they sat down together, and Childe Rowland told her all that he had done, and she told him how their two brothers had reached the Dark Tower, but had been enchanted by the King of Elfland, and lay there entombed as if dead. And then after they had talked a little longer Childe Rowland began to feel hungry from his long travels, and asked his sister for some food.

Burd Ellen looked at Childe Rowland sadly, but she was under a spell, and could not warn him, so she brought a golden basin full of bread and milk. Childe

Rowland was just going to raise it to his lips, when he remembered Merlin's warning. So he dashed the bowl to the ground, and said, "Not a drop will I swallow, nor a bit will I bite, till Burd Ellen is set free."

At that moment they heard the noise of someone approaching, and a loud voice was heard saying:

"*Fee, fi, fo, fum,*

I smell the blood of a Christian man,

Be he dead, be he living, with my brand,

I'll dash his brains from his brain-pan."

And then the folding doors of the hall were burst open, and the King of Elfland rushed in.

"Strike then, if you dare," shouted out Childe Rowland, and rushed to meet him with his good sword that never yet did fail. They fought, and they fought, till Childe Rowland beat the King of Elfland down on to his knees, and caused him to yield.

"I grant you mercy," said Childe Rowland, "release my sister from your spells and raise my brothers to life, and let us all go free, and you shall be spared."

"I agree," said the Elfin king, and rising up he went

to a chest from which he took a phial filled with a
blood-red liquor. With this he anointed the ears,
eyelids, nostrils, lips, and fingertips of the two
brothers, and they sprang at once into life, and
declared that their souls had been away, but had now
returned. The Elfin king then said some words to
Burd Ellen, and she was disenchanted, and they all
four passed out of the hall, through the long passage,
and turned their back on the Dark Tower, never to
return again. They reached home, and the good
queen, their mother, and Burd Ellen never went round
a church widershins again.

The Third Voyage
of Sinbad the Sailor

An extract from *The Arabian Nights Entertainments*,
retold by Andrew Lang

Long ago, a Middle Eastern man called Sinbad went to sea to
seek his fortune in strange lands. On his first voyage, he landed
on what appeared to be an island but was an enormous, sleeping
whale! When the whale dived, Sinbad was washed ashore on
another island. Here, he helped to save a king's horse from
drowning. The king rewarded Sinbad richly and he returned to
Baghdad wealthy. Soon restless, Sinbad set off on a second
voyage. Once accidentally abandoned by his shipmates, he found
himself stranded in a valley of diamonds. He was lifted out of
the valley by a gigantic bird called a roc, and returned to
Baghdad with a fortune in gems.

AFTER A VERY SHORT TIME the pleasant, easy life I led made me quite forget the perils of my two voyages. Moreover, as I was still in the prime of life, it pleased me better to be up and doing. So once more providing myself with the rarest and choicest merchandise of Baghdad, I set sail with other merchants of my acquaintance for distant lands. We had touched at many ports and made much profit, when one day upon the open sea we were caught by a terrible wind. Lasting for several days, it finally drove us into harbor on a strange island.

"I would rather have come to anchor anywhere than here," exclaimed our captain. "This island is inhabited by hairy savages, who are certain to attack us. Whatever these dwarfs may do we dare not resist, since they swarm like locusts, and if one of them is killed the rest will fall upon us, and speedily make an end of us."

Only too soon we were to find out that the captain spoke truly. There appeared a vast multitude of hideous savages, not more than two feet high and covered with reddish fur. Throwing themselves into the waves, they surrounded our vessel. Chattering in a language we could not understand, and clutching at ropes and gangways, they swarmed up the ship's side with such speed and agility that they almost seemed to fly.

You may imagine the rage and terror that seized us as we watched, unable to do anything to stop them. They sailed our vessel to an island that lay a little further off, where they drove us ashore; then they made off with our ship, leaving us helpless.

We wandered miserably inland, eating various herbs and fruits that we found as we went. Presently we saw in the distance what seemed to us to be a splendid palace, toward which we turned our weary steps. But when we reached it we saw that it was a castle, lofty, and strongly built. Pushing back the heavy, ebony doors we entered the courtyard, but upon the threshold of the great hall beyond it we paused, frozen with horror, at the sight which greeted us. On one side lay a huge pile of bones—human bones, and on the other numberless spits for roasting! Overcome with terror, we sank trembling to the ground and lay there in despair.

The sun was setting when a loud noise aroused us. The door of the hall was violently burst open and a horrible giant entered. He was as tall as a palm tree and had one eye, which flamed like a burning coal in the middle of his forehead. His teeth were long and sharp, while his lower lip hung down upon his chest. He had ears like an elephant's ears, which covered his shoulders, and nails like the claws of some fierce bird.

The giant examined us with his fearful eye, then came toward us, and grabbed me by the back of the neck, turning me this way and that. Feeling that I was mere skin and bone he set me down again and went on to the next, whom he treated in the same fashion; at last he came to the captain, and finding him the fattest, he stuck him upon a spit and kindled a huge fire at which he roasted him. After the giant had supped he lay down to sleep, snoring like the loudest thunder, while we lay shivering with horror

the whole night through.

When day broke he awoke and went out. Then we bemoaned our horrible fate, until the hall echoed with our despairing cries. Though we were many and our enemy was alone, no plan could we devise to escape from the island. So at last, submitting to our sad fate, we spent the day in wandering up and down the island eating what we could find. When night came we returned to the castle, having sought in vain for any other place of shelter.

At sunset the giant returned, supped upon one of our unhappy comrades, slept and snored till dawn, and then left us as before. Our condition seemed to us so frightful that several of my companions thought it would be better to leap from the cliffs and perish in the waves at once, rather than await so miserable an end; but at last I had an idea to combat the giant. I told it to my companions, then added, "Plenty of driftwood lies along the shore. Let us make several rafts. If our plot succeeds, we can wait patiently for some passing ship to rescue us. If it fails, we must quickly take to our rafts; frail as they are, we have more chance of saving our lives with them than we have if we remain here."

All agreed with me, and we spent the day building rafts, each capable of carrying three persons. At nightfall we returned to the castle, and very soon in came the giant, and one more of our number was sacrificed. But the time of our vengeance was at hand! As soon as he had finished his horrible repast he lay down to sleep as before, and when we heard him begin to snore I, and nine of the boldest of my comrades, rose softly and took a spit, which we made red-hot in the fire. Then at a given signal we plunged it into the giant's eye, completely blinding him. Uttering a terrible cry, he sprang to his feet clutching in all directions to try to seize one of us, but we had all fled different ways as soon as the deed was done, and thrown ourselves flat upon the ground in corners where he was not likely to touch us.

After a vain search he fumbled about till he found the door, and fled out of it howling frightfully. We

too fled from the castle and, stationing
ourselves beside our rafts, we waited to see
what would happen.

Alas! Morning light showed our enemy
approaching us, supported on either hand
by two giants nearly as large and fearful as
himself, while a crowd of others followed
close upon their heels. Hesitating no
longer we clambered upon our rafts and
rowed with all our might out to sea. The
giants seized up huge pieces of rock and,
wading into the water, hurled them after us
with such good aim that all the rafts except
the one I was upon were swamped, and
their luckless crews drowned. Indeed I and
my two companions had all we could do to
keep our own raft beyond the reach of the
giants. But by rowing hard we at last gained
the open sea.

The Third Voyage of Sinbad the Sailor

Jorinda and Jorindel

By the Brothers Grimm

THERE WAS ONCE an old castle that stood in the middle of a deep, gloomy wood, and in the castle lived an old fairy. Now this fairy could take any shape she pleased. All day long she flew about in the form of an owl, or crept about like a cat, but at night she always became an old woman again. When any young man came within a hundred paces of her castle, he became quite fixed, and could not move a step till she came and set him free; but when any pretty maiden came within that space she was changed into a bird, and the fairy put her into a cage, and hung her up in a chamber in the castle. There were seven hundred of these cages hanging in the castle, and all with beautiful birds in them.

Now there was once a maiden whose name was Jorinda. She was prettier than all the pretty girls that ever were seen before, and a shepherd lad, whose name was Jorindel, was in love with her, and they were soon to be married. One day they went for a walk in the wood and Jorindel said, "We must take care that we don't go too near to the fairy's castle."

It was a beautiful evening. The last rays of the setting sun shone bright through the long stems of the trees upon the green underwood beneath, and the turtledoves sang from the tall birches. Jorinda sat down to gaze upon the sun and Jorindel sat by her side. Both felt sad, they knew not why; but it seemed as if they were to be parted from one another for ever. They had wandered a long way, and when they looked to see which way they should go home, they found themselves at a loss to know what path to take.

The sun was setting fast. Jorindel suddenly looked

behind him, and saw through the bushes that they had, without knowing it, sat down close under the old walls of the castle. Then he shrank for fear, turned pale, and trembled.

Jorinda was just singing, when her song stopped suddenly. Jorindel turned to see the reason, and beheld his Jorinda changed into a nightingale! Jorindel could not move, he stood fixed as a stone, and could neither weep, nor speak, nor stir hand or foot.

And now the sun went quite down, the gloomy night came, and the old fairy came forth pale and meager, with staring eyes, and a nose and chin that almost met one another. She mumbled something to herself, seized the nightingale, and went away with it in her hand.

Poor Jorindel saw the nightingale was gone—but what could he do? He could not speak, he could not move from the spot where he stood. At last the fairy came back and suddenly Jorindel found himself free. Then he fell on his knees before the fairy, and begged her to give him back his dear Jorinda, but she laughed at him, and said he would never see her again. Then she went on her way.

He prayed, he wept, he sorrowed, but all in vain.

Alas!" he said. "What will become of me?" He could not go back to his own home, so he went to a nearby village, and employed himself in keeping sheep. Many a time did he walk round and round as near to the hated castle as he dared go, but all in vain. He heard or saw nothing of Jorinda.

At last he dreamed one night that he found a beautiful purple flower, and that in the middle of it lay an expensive pearl; and he dreamed that he plucked the flower, and went with it in his hand into the castle, and that everything he touched with it was disenchanted, and that there he found his Jorinda.

In the morning when he awoke, he began to search over hill and dale for this pretty flower, and eight long days he sought for it in vain. But on the ninth day, early in the morning, he found the beautiful purple flower, and in the middle of it was a large dewdrop, as big as an expensive pearl. Then he plucked the flower, and traveled day and night, till he came again to the castle. He walked nearer than a hundred paces to it, and yet he did not become fixed as before, but found that he could go quite close up to the door. Jorindel was very glad indeed to see this. Then he touched the door with the flower, and it sprang open, so he went in through the court and listened, hearing many birds singing.

At last he came to the chamber where the fairy sat, with the seven hundred birds singing in the seven hundred cages. When the fairy saw Jorindel she was very angry and screamed with rage, but she could not come within two yards of him, for the flower he held in his hand was his safeguard. He looked around at the birds in the cages, but there were many, many nightingales. How then should he find out which one was his Jorinda?

While he was thinking what to do, he saw the fairy had taken down one of the cages, and was making her way off through the door. He ran after her, touched the cage with the flower, and Jorinda stood before him, and threw her arms round his neck looking as beautiful as ever, as beautiful as when they walked together in the wood.

Then he touched all the other birds with the flower, so that they all took their old forms again. And he took Jorinda home, where they were married, and lived happily together for many years. And so did a good many other lads, whose maidens had been forced to sing in the old fairy's cages by themselves, much longer than they liked.

The History of Jack the Giant-Killer

From Andrew Lang's *Blue Fairy Book*

IN THE REIGN of the famous King Arthur there lived in Cornwall a lad named Jack, who was a boy of a bold temper. He took delight in hearing or reading of conjurers, giants, and fairies, and used to listen eagerly to the deeds of the knights of King Arthur's Round Table.

In those days there lived on St Michael's Mount, off Cornwall, a huge giant, eighteen meters high and nine meters round. His fierce and savage looks were the terror of all who beheld him.

He dwelled in a gloomy cavern on the top of the

mountain, and used to wade over to the mainland in search of prey. He would throw half a dozen oxen upon his back, and tie three times as many sheep and hogs round his waist, and march back to his abode.

The giant had done this for many years when Jack resolved to destroy him. Jack took a horn, a shovel, a pickax, his armor, and a dark lantern, and one winter's evening he went to the mount. There he dug a pit twenty-two meters deep and twenty broad. He covered the top over so as to make it look like solid ground. He then blew his horn so loudly that the giant awoke and came out of his den crying out, "You villain! You shall pay for this! I'll broil you for my breakfast!" He had just finished, when, taking one step further, he tumbled into the pit, and Jack struck him a blow on the head with his pickax, which killed him. Jack then returned home to cheer his friends with the news.

Another giant, called Blunderbore, vowed to be revenged on Jack if ever he should have him in his power. This giant lived in an enchanted castle in a lonely wood and one day came across Jack lying under a tree in the wood, asleep. The giant carried Jack off to his castle, where he locked him up in a large room, the floor of which was covered with the bodies, skulls, and bones of men and women.

Soon afterward the giant went to fetch his brother, to take a meal of Jack's flesh. Jack saw with terror through the bars of his prison the two giants approaching. Then he noticed in one corner of the room a strong rope. He took courage and, making a slip knot at each end, threw them over their heads, and tied it to the window bars, then he pulled till he had choked them. When they were dead, he slid down the rope.

Jack next took a great bunch of keys from the

pocket of Blunderbore, and went into the castle
again. He searched through all the rooms, and in one
of them found three ladies tied up by the hair and
almost starved to death. They told him that their
husbands had been killed by the giants, who had then
condemned them to be starved to death.

"Ladies," said Jack, "I have put an end to the
monster and his wicked brother, and I give you this
castle and all the riches it contains, to make some
amends for the dreadful pains you have felt." He then
very politely gave them the keys of the castle.

Having hitherto been successful in all his
undertakings, Jack resolved not to be idle in future.
He therefore furnished himself with a horse, a cap of
knowledge, a sword of sharpness, shoes of swiftness,
and an invisible coat, the better to perform the
wonderful enterprises that lay before him.

He traveled over hills and dales till, arriving at the
foot of a high mountain, he knocked at the door of a
lonely house. An old man let him in, and when Jack
was seated, the old man said, "My son, on the top of

this mountain is an enchanted castle, kept by the giant Galligantus and a vile magician. They seized a duke's daughter, as she was walking in her father's garden, and then they brought her here transformed into a deer."

Jack promised that in the morning, at the risk of his life, he would break the enchantment, and after a sound sleep he rose early, put on his invisible coat, and got ready for the attempt.

When he had climbed to the top of the mountain he saw two fiery griffins, but he passed between them without the least fear of danger, for they could not see him because of his invisible coat. On the castle gate he found a golden trumpet, under which were written these lines:

> Whoever can this trumpet blow
> Shall cause the giant's overthrow.

As soon as Jack had read this he seized the trumpet and blew a shrill blast, which made the gates fly open and the very castle itself tremble.

The giant and the magician now knew that their

wicked course was at an end, and they stood biting their thumbs and shaking with fear. Jack, with his sword of sharpness, soon killed the giant, and the magician was then carried away by a whirlwind; and every knight and beautiful lady who had been changed into birds and beasts returned to their proper shapes. The castle vanished away like smoke, and the head of the giant Galligantus was then sent to King Arthur.

The knights and ladies rested that night at the old man's house, and next day they set out for the Court. Jack's fame had now spread through the whole country, and the duke gave him his daughter in marriage. After this the king gave him a large estate, on which he and his lady lived the rest of their days in joy and contentment.

Tamlane

From *More English Fairy Tales,*
by Joseph Jacobs

YOUNG TAMLANE was son of Earl Murray, and Burd Janet was daughter of Dunbar, Earl of March. And when they were young they loved one another and vowed to get married. But when the time came near for their marrying, Tamlane disappeared, and none knew what had become of him.

Many, many days after he had disappeared, Burd Janet was wandering in Carterhaugh Wood, though she had been warned not to go there. She came to a bush of broom and began plucking it. She had not taken more than three flowers when by her side appeared young Tamlane.

"Where have you from, Tamlane?" Burd Janet said. "And why have you been away so long?"

"From Elfland I come," said young Tamlane. "The Queen of Elfland has made me her knight."

"But how did you get there?" asked Burd Janet.

"I was hunting one day, and as I rode in the opposite direction to the sun, a deep drowsiness fell upon me, and when I awoke, behold! I was in Elfland."

"Oh, tell me if anything I can do will save you?"

"Tomorrow night is Halloween, and the fairy court will then ride through England and Scotland, and if you would rescue me from Elfland you must stand by Miles Cross between twelve and one at night, and cast holy water all around you."

"But how shall I know you, Tamlane," cried Burd Janet, "amid so many knights I've never seen before?"

"The first court of elves that come by, let them pass. The next court you shall curtsey to, but do nothing or say anything. But the third court that comes by is the chief court, and at the head rides the Queen of Elfland. And I shall ride by her side upon a milk-white steed with a star in my crown. Watch my hands, the right one will be gloved but the left one bare, and you will know that is me."

"But how will I save you?" asked Burd Janet.

"You must spring upon me suddenly, and I will fall to the ground. Then seize me quick, and whatever change befalls me, for they will exercise all their magic on me, cling on till they turn me into red-hot iron. Then cast me into the water and I will be turned back into a man. Then cast your green mantle over me, and I shall be yours, and be of the world again."

So Burd Janet promised to do all this for Tamlane, and the next night at midnight she took her place by Miles Cross and cast holy water around her.

Soon there came riding by the Elfin Court, first over the mound went a troop on black steeds, and then another troop on brown. But in the third court, all on milk-white steeds, she saw the Queen of

Elfland, and by her side a knight with
a star in his crown, with his right
hand gloved and the left bare.
Then she knew this was
Tamlane, and springing
forward she seized the bridle
of the milk-white steed and
pulled its rider down. As
soon as he had touched the
ground she let go of the
bridle and seized Tamlane in
her arms.

"He's won, he's won
amongst us all," shrieked out
the strange crew, and all gathered
around her and tried their spells
on Tamlane.

First they turned him in Janet's
arms like frozen ice, then into a flame
of roaring fire. Then, again, the fire
vanished and an adder was in her arms,

but still she held on; and then they turned him into a snake that reared up as if to bite her, and yet she held on. Then suddenly a dove was struggling in her arms, and almost flew away. Then they turned him into a swan, but all was in vain, till at last he was turned into red-hot iron, and this she cast into a well of water and then he turned back into a man. She quickly cast her green mantle over him, and young Tamlane was Burd Janet's. And the Elfin Court rode away, and Burd Janet and young Tamlane went their way homeward and were married soon afterward.

The Twelve Brothers

Retold by Andrew Lang in his *Red Fairy Book*,
after the Brothers Grimm

THERE WAS ONCE UPON A TIME a king and a queen who had twelve children, all of whom were boys. One day the king said to his wife, "If our thirteenth child is a girl, all her twelve brothers must die, so that the kingdom may be hers alone."

Then he ordered twelve coffins to be made, and put these away in an empty room and, giving the key to his wife, he bade her tell no one of it.

The queen grieved and refused to be comforted, so much so that the youngest boy, who was always with her, and whom she had christened Benjamin, said to her one day: "Dear Mother, why are you so sad?"

"My child," she answered, "I cannot tell you."

But Benjamin left her no peace, till she went and unlocked the room and showed him the twelve little coffins and explained. She wept bitterly, but her son

comforted her and said, "Don't cry, dear Mother, we'll escape somehow."

"Yes," replied his mother, "that is what you must do—go with your eleven brothers out into the wood. Let one of you always sit on the highest tree you can find, keeping watch on the tower of the castle. If I give birth to a little son I will wave a white flag, and then you may safely return; but if I give birth to a little daughter I will wave a red flag, which will warn you to fly away as quickly as you can. Every night I will get up and pray for you."

Then she blessed her sons and they set out into the wood. They found a very high oak tree, and there they sat, keeping their eyes always fixed on the castle tower. On the twelfth day, when the turn came to Benjamin, he noticed a flag waving in the air, but alas! It was not white, but blood red, the sign that told them they must all die. When the brothers heard this they were very angry, and said, "Shall we suffer death for the sake of a wretched girl? Let us vow that wherever and whenever we meet a female, she shall die at our hands."

Then they went their way deeper into the wood, and in the middle of it, where it was thickest and darkest, they came upon a little enchanted house that stood empty.

"Here," they said, "let us take up our abode, and you, Benjamin, you shall stay at home and keep house

for us; we will go out and fetch food." So they went
forth into the wood and foraged and hunted. So they
lived for ten years in this little house, and the time
slipped merrily away.

Meantime, their little sister grew up kind-hearted
and of a fair countenance, with a gold star right in
the middle of her forehead. One day the girl looked
down from her window and saw twelve men's shirts
hanging on the washing line to dry, and asked her
mother, "Who do these shirts belong to? Surely they
are far too small for my father?"

And the queen answered sadly, "Dear child, they
belong to your twelve brothers."

"But where are my twelve brothers?" said the girl.
"I have never even heard of them."

"Heaven alone knows!" replied her mother. Then
she took the girl and opened the locked-up room and
showed her the twelve coffins.

The queen told all that had happened, and when
she had finished her daughter said, "Do not cry,
dearest Mother. I will go and seek my brothers till I

find them." So she took the twelve shirts and went on straight into the middle of the big wood. She walked all day long, and came in the evening to the little enchanted house. She stepped in and found a youth who, marveling at her beauty, at the royal robes she wore, and at the golden star on her forehead, asked her where she came from and where she was going.

"I am a princess," she answered, "and am seeking my twelve brothers. I mean to wander as far as the blue sky stretches over the earth till I find them."

Then she showed him the twelve shirts that she had taken with her, and Benjamin saw that it must be his sister, and said, "I am your youngest brother."

So they wept for joy, and hugged each other.

After a time Benjamin said: "Dear sister, there is still a problem, for we had all agreed that any girl we met should die at our hands, because it was for the sake of a girl that we had to leave our kingdom. Go and hide under that tub till our eleven brothers come in, and I'll make matters right with them."

She did as she was bid, and soon the others came

home from the chase and sat down to supper.

"Well, well," Benjamin said to his brothers, "you've been out in the wood all the day and I've stayed quietly at home, and yet I've got exciting news!"

"Then tell us," they cried.

But he answered, "Only on condition that you promise faithfully that the first girl we meet shall not be killed."

"She shall be spared," they promised, "only tell us the news."

Then Benjamin said: "Our sister is here!" and he lifted up the tub and the princess stepped forward, with her royal robes and with the golden star on her forehead, looking so lovely and sweet and charming that they all loved her on the spot.

They arranged that she should stay at home with Benjamin and help him in the housework, while the rest of the brothers went out into the wood to forage and hunt. The princess made herself so generally useful that her brothers were delighted, and they all lived happily together.

One day the two at home prepared a fine feast, and when they were all assembled they sat down and ate and drank and made merry. Now there was a little garden around the enchanted house, in which grew twelve tall lilies. The girl, wishing to please her brothers, started to pluck the twelve flowers, meaning to present one to each of them after supper. But hardly had she begun when her brothers were turned into twelve ravens, who flew croaking over the wood, and the house and garden vanished also.

So the poor girl found herself left all alone in the wood, and as she looked round her she noticed an old woman standing close by, who said, "My child, what have you done? Why didn't you leave the flowers alone? Now your brothers are

201

changed forever into ravens."

The girl asked, sobbing, "Is there no means of setting them free?"

"There is only one way," said the old woman, "and that is so difficult that you won't free them by it, for you would have to be dumb and not laugh for seven years, and if you spoke a single word it would slay your brothers."

Then the girl said to herself, "If that is all, I am quite sure I can free my brothers." So she searched for a high tree, and climbed up it and spun all day long, never laughing nor speaking one word.

Now it happened one day that a king who was out hunting had a greyhound, who ran sniffing to the tree on which the girl sat, and jumped round it, yelping and barking furiously. When the king looked up and beheld the beautiful princess with the golden star on her forehead, he was so enchanted that he asked her to be his wife. She gave no answer, but nodded slightly. Then he climbed up the tree, lifted her down, and bore her home to his palace. The marriage was celebrated with much ceremony, but the bride neither spoke nor laughed.

When they had lived a few years happily together, the king's mother, who was a wicked old woman, began to speak ill of the young queen, accusing her of many evil things. Of course, the queen could not speak for herself to protest, and eventually the king let himself be talked over, and condemned his beautiful wife to death.

So a great fire was lit in the courtyard of the palace, where she was to be burned, and the king watched from an upper window, crying bitterly, for

he still loved his wife dearly. But just as she had been bound to the stake, and the flames were licking her garments, the very last moment of the seven years came. Then a sudden rushing sound was heard and twelve ravens swooped downward. As soon as they touched the ground they turned into her twelve brothers, and she knew that she had freed them. They quenched the flames and, unbinding their dear sister from the stake, they kissed and hugged her again and again. Now that she was able to speak, she told the king why she had been dumb and not able to laugh.

The king rejoiced greatly when he heard she was innocent, and they all lived happily ever after.

LITTLE VILLAINS AND EVIL MONSTERS

Tom Tit Tot

A Rumpelstiltskin story,
retold by Joseph Jacobs in *English Fairy Tales*

ONCE UPON A TIME there was a woman who
baked five pies. When they came out of the
oven, they were that overbaked the crusts were too
hard to eat. So she says to her daughter, "Put them
there pies on the shelf, and leave 'em there a little, and
they'll come again." She meant that the crust would
get soft.

But the girl, said to herself, "Well, if they'll come
again, I'll eat 'em now." And she set to work and ate
'em all, first and last.

Come suppertime the woman said, "Go you, and

get one o' them there pies. I dare say they've come again now."

The girl went and she looked, and there was nothing but the dishes. So back she came and said, "Noo, they ain't come again."

"Not one of 'em?" says the mother.

"Not one of 'em," says she.

"Well, come again, or not come again," said the woman, "I'll have one for supper."

"But you can't, if they ain't come," said the girl.

"But I can," says she. "Go you, and bring the best of 'em."

"Best or worst," says the girl, "I've ate 'em all, and you can't have one till that's come again."

Well, the woman she was done, and she took her spinning to the door, and as she span she sang:

"My daughter ate five, five pies today.

My daughter ate five, five pies today."

The king was coming down the street, and he heard her sing, but what she sang he couldn't hear, so he stopped and said, "What was that you were singing, my good woman?"

The woman was ashamed to let him hear what her daughter had been doing, so she instead she sang:

"My daughter has spun five, five skeins today.

My daughter has spun five, five skeins today."

"Stars o' mine!" said the king, "I never heard tell of anyone that could do that."

Then he said, "I want a wife, and I'll marry your daughter. But look you here," says he, "eleven months out of the year she shall have all she likes to eat, and all the gowns she likes to get, and all the company she likes to keep; but the last month of the year she'll have to spin five skeins every day, and if she don't, I shall kill her."

"All right," says the woman; for she thought what a grand marriage that was. And as for the five skeins, when the time came, there'd be plenty of ways of getting out of it, and likeliest, he'd have forgotten all about it.

So they were married. And for eleven months the girl had all she liked to eat, and all the gowns she liked to get, and all the company she liked to keep.

But when the time was getting over, she began to think about the skeins and to wonder if he had 'em in mind. But not one word did he say about 'em, and she thought he'd wholly forgotten 'em.

However, the last day of the last month he takes her to a room she'd never set eyes on before. There was nothing in it but a spinning wheel and a stool. And says he, "Now, my dear, here you'll be shut in tomorrow with some food and drink and some flax, and if you haven't spun five skeins by the night, your head'll be cut off." And away he went about his business.

Well, she was that frightened, she'd always been such a careless girl, that she didn't so much as know how to spin, and what was she to do tomorrow with no one to come to help her? She sat down on a stool in the kitchen, and lord, how she did cry!

However, all of a sudden she heard a sort of knocking low down on the door. She upped and opened it, and what should she see but a little imp

with a long tail, that looked up at her
curiously, and said, "Why are you a-crying?"

"What's that to you?" says she.

"Never you mind," said the imp, "but
tell me what you're a-crying for."

"That won't do me no good if I do,"
says she.

"You don't know that,"
it said, and twirled its tail
around.

"Well," says she, "that won't do no harm, if that don't do no good," and she told about the pies, and the skeins, and everything.

"This is what I'll do," says the little imp, "I'll come to your window every morning and take the flax and bring it spun at night."

"What's your pay?" says she.

The imp looked out the corner of its eyes, and said, "I'll give you three chances every night to guess my name, and if you haven't guessed it before the month's up, you shall be mine."

Well, she thought she'd be sure to guess the name before the month was up. "All right," says she, "I agree."

"All right," the imp says, and lord, how it twirled its tail!

Well, the next day, the king took the girl into the room, and there was the flax and the day's food. "Now there's the flax," says he, and if that ain't spun this night, off goes your head." And then he went out and locked the door.

He'd hardly gone, when there was a knocking against the window. She upped and she opened it, and there sure enough was the little imp sitting on the ledge.

"Where's the flax?" it says.

"Here it be," says she, and she gave it to the imp.

Well, come the evening a knocking came again to the window. She upped and she opened it, and there was the little imp with five skeins of flax on its arm. "Here it be," and it gave it to her. "Now, what's my name?" it says.

"What, is that Bill?" says she.

"Noo, that ain't," says it, and it twirled its tail.

"Is that Ned?" says she.

"Noo, that ain't," says it, and it twirled its tail.

"Well, is that Mark?" says she.

"Noo, that ain't," says it, and it twirled its tail harder, and away it flew.

Well, when her husband came in, there were the five skeins ready for him. "I see I shan't have to kill you tonight, my dear," says he; "you'll have your food and

your flax in the morning," and away he goes.

Well every day the flax and the food were brought, and every day that there little imp used to come mornings and evenings. And all the day the girl sat trying to think of names to say to it when it came at night. But she never hit on the right one. And as it got toward the end of the month, the imp began to look so full of malice, and it twirled its tail faster and faster each time she gave a guess.

At last it came to the last day but one. The imp came at night along with the five skeins, and said,

"What, ain't you got my name yet?"

"Is that Nicodemus?" says she.

"Noo, it ain't," it says.

"Is that Sammle?" says she.

"Noo, it ain't," it says.

"A-well, is that Methusalem?" says she.

"Noo, it ain't that neither," it says.

Then it looks at her with its eyes like a coal o' fire, and says: "Woman, there's only tomorrow night, and then you'll be mine!" And away it flew.

Well, she felt horrid. However, she heard the king coming along the passage.

In he came, and when he sees the five skeins, he says, "Well, my dear, I don't see but what you'll have your skeins ready tomorrow night as well, and as I reckon I shan't have to kill you, I'll have supper in here tonight." So they brought supper, and another stool for him, and down the two sat.

Well, he hadn't eaten but a mouthful or so, when he stops and begins to laugh.

"What is it?" says she.

"A-why," says he, "I was out a-hunting today, and I got away to a place in the wood I'd never seen before. And there was an old chalk pit. And I heard a sort of humming. So I got off my horse, and I went quietly to the pit, and I looked down. Well, what should there be but the funniest little imp you ever set eyes on. And what was it doing but it had a little spinning wheel, and it was spinning wonderful fast, and twirling its tail. And as it span that sang:

'Nimmy nimmy not

Tom Tit Tot

My name's Tom Tit Tot'."

Well, when the girl heard this, she felt as if she
could have jumped out her skin for joy, but she didn't
say a word.

My name's Tom Tit Tot'."

Well, when the girl heard this, she felt as if she
could have jumped out her skin for joy, but she didn't
say a word.

My name's Tom Tit Tot'."

Well, when the girl heard this, she felt as if she could have jumped out her skin for joy, but she didn't say a word.

217

Next day that there little imp looked so full of malice when it came for the flax. And when night came, she heard it knocking against the window panes. She opened the window, and it came right in on the ledge. It was grinning from ear to ear, and ooh, its tail was twirling round so fast!

"What's my name?" it says.

"Is that Solomon?" she says.

"Noo, it aint," it says, and it came further into the room.

"Well, is that Zebedee?" says she again.

"Noo, it aint," says the imp. And then it laughed and twirled its tail till you couldn't hardly see it.

"Take your time, woman," it says; "because next guess, and you're mine." And it stretched out its hands at her.

Well, she backed a step or two, and she looked at it, and then she laughed out, and says she, pointing her finger at it:

"Nimmy nimmy not
    Your name's Tom Tit Tot."

Well, when it heard her, the imp gave an awful
shriek and away it flew into the dark, and she never
saw it anymore.

The Story of the Fisherman

From *The Arabian Nights Entertainments,*
retold by Andrew Lang

THERE WAS, ONCE UPON A TIME, a fisherman so old and poor that he could scarcely manage to support his wife and children. He went every day to fish very early—one morning he started out by moonlight. He threw his nets and as he was drawing them in he felt a great weight. He thought he had caught a large fish, and he felt very pleased. But a moment afterward, seeing that he had in his nets only the carcass of an donkey, he was much disappointed.

Vexed, he threw his nets in a second time. In drawing them in he again felt a great weight, so that

he thought they were full of fish. But he found only
a large basket full of garbage. He was much annoyed.
"O Fortune," he cried, "do not trifle thus with me, a
poor fisherman, who can hardly support his family!"

So saying, he threw his nets in for the third time.
But he only drew in stones, shells, and mud. He was
almost in despair.

Then he threw his nets for the fourth time. When
he thought he had a fish he drew them in with a great
deal of trouble. There was no fish, but he found a
yellow vase, which by its weight seemed full of
something, and he noticed that it was fastened and
sealed with lead, with the impression of a seal. The
fisherman was delighted. "I will sell it," he said, "and
with the money I shall get for it I shall buy a measure
of wheat."

He examined the vase on all sides; he shook it to
see if it would rattle. But he heard nothing, and so,
judging from the impression of the seal and the lid,
he thought there must be something precious inside.
To find out, he took his knife, and with a little

trouble he opened it. He turned it upside down, but nothing came out, which surprised him very much. He set it in front of him, and whilst he was looking at it attentively, such a thick smoke came out that he had to step back a pace or two. This smoke rose up to the clouds and, stretching over the sea and the shore, formed a thick mist, which caused the fisherman much astonishment. When all the smoke was out of the vase it gathered itself together, and became a thick mass in which appeared a genie, twice as large as the largest giant. When he saw such

a terrible-looking
monster, the
fisherman would
liked to have run
away, but he
trembled so with
fright that he could
not move a step.

"Great king of
the genies," cried
the large monster,
"I will never again
disobey you!"

And at these
words the fisherman
took great courage.

"What is this you are
saying, genie? Tell me
how you came to be shut
up in that vase."

At this, the genie looked at

the fisherman haughtily. "Speak to me more civilly," he said, "before I kill you."

"Alas! Why should you kill me?" cried the fisherman. "I have just freed you; have you already forgotten that?"

"No," answered the genie; "but that will not prevent me from killing you; and I am only going to grant you one favor, and that is to choose the manner of your death."

"What have I done to you?" asked the fisherman.

"I cannot treat you in any other way," said the genie, "and if you would know why, listen to my story. I rebelled against the king of the genies. To punish me, he shut me up in this vase of copper, and he put on the leaden seal, which is enchantment enough to prevent my coming out. Then he had the vase thrown into the sea. During the first period of my captivity I vowed that if anyone should free me before a hundred years were passed, I would make him rich even after his death. But that century passed, and no one freed me. In the second century I vowed that I would give all the treasures in the world to my deliverer; but he never came. In the third, I promised to make him a king, to be always near him, and to grant him three wishes every day; but that century passed away as the other two had done, and I remained in the same plight. At last I grew angry at being captive for so long, and I vowed that if anyone would release me I would kill him at once, and would only allow him to choose in what manner he should die. So you see, as you have freed me today, choose in what way you will die."

The fisherman was very unhappy. "What an unlucky man I am to have freed you! I implore you to spare my life."

"I have told you," said the genie, "that it is impossible. Choose quickly; you are wasting time."

The fisherman began to devise a plot.

"Since I must die," he said, "before I choose the manner of my death, I conjure you on your honor to tell me if you really were in that vase?"

"Yes, I was," answered the genie.

"I really cannot believe it," said the fisherman. "That vase could not contain one of your feet even, and how could your whole body go in? I cannot believe it unless I see you do it."

Then the genie began to change himself into smoke, which, as before, spread over the sea and the shore, and which, then collecting itself together, began to go back into the vase slowly and evenly till there was nothing left outside. Then a voice came from the vase which said to the fisherman, "Well, unbelieving fisherman, here I am in the vase; do you believe me now?"

The fisherman, instead of answering, took the lid of lead and shut it down quickly on the vase.

"Now, O genie," he cried, "ask pardon of me, and choose by what death you will die! But no, it will be better if I throw you into the sea whence I drew you out, and I will build a house on the shore to warn fishermen who come to cast their nets here, against fishing up such a wicked genie as you are, who vows to kill the man who frees you."

At these words the genie did all he could to get out, but he could not, because of the enchantment of the lid.

Jack in Wales

By Flora Annie Steel

ONCE UPON A TIME, Jack, the famous Giant Killer, found himself lost in wild Wales, far from any human house. As night fell he wandered on, until, on entering a narrow valley, he came to a very large, dreary-looking house, almost a castle, standing alone.

Being anxious for shelter Jack went up to the door and knocked. You may imagine his surprise and alarm when the summons was answered by a giant with two heads. However, though this giant's look was very fierce, his manners were quite polite. The truth was that he was an evil giant. He appeared friendly because this was how he tried to win people over, by a show of false friendship.

So he welcomed Jack heartily in a strong Welsh accent and prepared a bedroom for him, where he was left with kind wishes for a good rest.

However, Jack was too tired to sleep well and, as he lay awake, he overheard the giant muttering to himself in the next room. Jack had very keen ears and he was able to make out these words, or something like them:

"Though here you lodge with me this night,
    You shall not see the morning light.
    My club shall dash your brains outright."

"Do you say!" said Jack, starting up at once. "So that is your trick, is it? But I will be even with you." Then, leaving his bed, Jack laid a big piece of wood among the blankets and, taking one of these to keep himself warm, made himself snug in a corner of the room. He pretended to snore, so as to make the giant think he was asleep.

And sure enough, in came the giant on tiptoe,
carrying a big club. Then—

WHACK! WHACK! WHACK!

Jack could hear the bed being beaten
until the giant, thinking every
bone of his guest's
body must be

broken, went out of the room
again. Then Jack went calmly to bed once more
and slept soundly.

Next morning the giant couldn't believe his eyes

when he saw Jack coming down the stairs fresh and hearty.

"Odds splutter hur nails!" he cried astonished. "Did you sleep well? Was there nothing you felt in the night?"

"Oh," replied Jack, laughing in his sleeve, "I think a rat did come and give me two or three flaps of his tail."

The giant was dumbfounded. He led Jack to breakfast, brought him a bowl that held at least four gallons of porridge, and told him to eat the lot.

When Jack was traveling he wore a leather bag under his cloak to carry his things and, as it happened, he still had it with him. So, quick as thought, he hitched it round in front with the opening just under his chin.

Then he set to work at the mighty bowl, filled to the brim with gray, lumpy porridge. As he spooned up the mixture, he slipped the best part of it into the leather bag without the giant being any the wiser.

So they sat down to breakfast, the giant gobbling down his own measure of porridge, while Jack carried on with his.

"Now see," says crafty Jack when he had finished. "I'll show you a trick," and with that he stood up with a carving-knife, ripped up the leather bag and out fell all the porridge on the floor!

"Odds splutter hur nails!" cried the giant. Not to be outdone, he said, "I can do that myself!" He

Jack in Wales

seized the carving-knife, ripped open his own belly and fell down dead.

And so Jack got rid of the Welsh giant.

Thirteenth

By Thomas Frederick Crane

T HERE WAS ONCE a father who had thirteen sons, the youngest of whom was named Thirteenth. The father had to work very hard to support his children, but he made what little money he could by gathering herbs.

One day, the King sent out a notice in the city that the person who would go and steal the ogre's bed covering would receive a reward of gold. Thirteenth's brothers went to the King and said, "Majesty, we have a brother named Thirteenth, who is bold enough to do that and other things too."

The King said, "Bring him to me at once."

They brought Thirteenth, who said, "Majesty, how is it possible to steal the ogre's bed covering? If he sees me he will eat me!"

"No matter, you must go," said the King. "I know that you are bold."

So Thirteenth went to the house of the ogre, who was away. The ogress was in the kitchen. Thirteenth entered the ogre's house quietly and hid himself under the bed.

At night, the ogre returned. He ate his supper and went to bed, saying as he did so, "I smell the smell of human flesh. When I see it, I will eat it!"

The ogress replied, "Be still, of course no one has entered here."

The ogre began to snore, and Thirteenth pulled the bed covering a little. But the ogre woke up and called out, "What is that?"

Thirteenth began to mew like a cat.

The ogress said, "Scat! Scat!" and clapped her hands. She then fell asleep again with the ogre.

Thirteenth gave a hard pull, seized the bed covering, and ran away.

The King was so pleased with the bed covering that he sent out another notice in the city: he would give a measure of gold to whoever brought him the ogre's pillow.

Thirteenth said, "Majesty, how is it possible to steal the ogre's pillow? The pillow is full of little bells, and you must know that the ogre awakens at the slightest breath."

"I know nothing about it," said the King. "I just want to have the pillow."

So Thirteenth departed, entered the house of the ogre, and crept under the ogre's bed. At midnight he stretched out his hand very softly, but the little bells all sounded.

"What is that?" said the ogre.

"Nothing," replied the ogress, "perhaps it is the wind that makes them ring."

But the ogre, who was suspicious, pretended to sleep, but kept his ears open.

Then Thirteenth stretched out his hand again. Alas! The ogre put out his arm and seized him.

"Now you are caught! Just wait, I will have you for my supper." Then he put Thirteenth in a barrel. The ogre began to feed him on raisins and figs to get him fat enough to make a fine feast for him and his wife.

After a time, the ogre said, "Stick out your finger, little Thirteenth, so that I can see whether you are fat." Thirteenth saw a mouse's tail and stuck that out.

"Ah, how thin you are!" said the ogre. "Eat, my son. Take the raisins and figs, and get fat soon!"

After some days the ogre told him again

to put out his finger and Thirteenth stuck out a splinter of wood. "Eh, wretch! Are you still so skinny? Eat, eat, and get fat soon."

At the end of the month, Thirteenth had nothing more to stick out, and had to show his finger. The ogre cried out in joy, "He is fat, he is fat! Quick, my ogress, heat the oven for three nights and three days, for I am going to invite our relatives, and we will make a fine banquet of Thirteenth."

Then the ogress heated the oven for three days and three nights. When she let Thirteenth out of the barrel, she said to him, "Come here, Thirteenth. You are going to help me put the lamb in the oven."

But Thirteenth knew what she was planning, and when he approached the oven he said, "Ah, mother ogress, what is that black thing in the corner of the oven?" The ogress stooped down a little but saw nothing.

"Stoop down again," said Thirteenth, "so that you can see it." When the

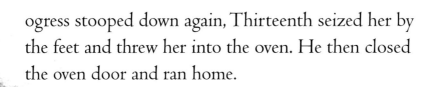

ogress stooped down again, Thirteenth seized her by
the feet and threw her into the oven. He then closed
the oven door and ran home.

After this, the King said to Thirteenth, "Listen, Thirteenth. To complete your brave tasks, I want you to bring me the ogre himself, alive and well."

"How can I, Your Majesty?" said Thirteenth. But he thought awhile, then added, "I will have a try."

Thirteenth had a strong chest made, and disguised himself with a long, false beard. He went to the ogre's house and called out to him, "Do you know Thirteenth? The wretch! He has killed some of my brothers, but I'll catch him! And when I catch him, I will shut him up in this chest!"

At these words the ogre drew near and said, "I, too, would like to help you, for you don't know what Thirteenth has done to me." And the ogre began to tell his story.

The pretending old man said, "I do not know Thirteenth. Do you know him?"

"Yes, sir."

"Then tell me, how tall is he?"

"As tall as I am."

"If that is so," said Thirteenth, "let us see whether

this chest will hold him. If it will hold you, it will hold him."

"Oh, good idea!" said the ogre, and he got into the chest. Then Thirteenth shut the chest and nailed it up, put it on a cart and went back to the city.

When he arrived, the King had an iron chain attached to the ogre's hands and feet, and made him gnaw bones for the rest of his miserable life. The King gave Thirteenth a huge pile of riches and treasures, and asked him always to stay by his side.

The Prince and the Dragon

From Andrew Lang's *Crimson Fairy Book*

ONCE UPON A TIME there lived an emperor who had three sons. They were all fine young men, who were very fond of hunting, and scarcely a day passed without one or other of them going out to look for game.

One morning the eldest mounted his horse and set out for a forest where wild animals of all sorts were to be found. He had not long left the castle, when a hare sprang out of a thicket and dashed across the road in front. The young man gave chase over hill and dale, till at last the hare took refuge in a mill by the

244

side of a river. The prince followed and entered the mill, but stopped in terror by the door, for, instead of a hare, before him stood a dragon, breathing flames. At this fearful sight the prince turned to fly, but a fiery tongue coiled round his waist, and drew him into the dragon's mouth, and he was seen no more.

A week passed, and when the prince never came back everyone in the town began to grow uneasy. At last his next brother told the emperor that he likewise would go out to hunt, and that perhaps he would find some clue as to his brother's disappearance. Hardly had the castle gates closed than the hare sprang out of the bushes as before, and led the huntsman up hill and down dale, till they reached the mill. Into this the hare flew with the prince at his heels, when, lo! Instead of the hare, there stood a dragon breathing flames; and out shot a fiery tongue that coiled round the prince's waist, and lifted him into the dragon's mouth, and he was seen no more.

Days went by, and the emperor waited for the sons who never came, and could not sleep at night for

wondering what had become of them. His youngest
son wished to go in search of his brothers, but for a
long time the emperor refused to listen, lest he should
lose him also. But the prince begged so hard, and
promised so often that he would be very careful, that
at length the emperor agreed.

Full of hope the young prince started on his way,
but no sooner was he outside the city than a hare
sprang out of the bushes and ran before him, till they
reached the mill. As before, the animal dashed
through the open door, but this time he was not
followed by the prince. Wiser than his brothers, the
young man turned away, saying, "There are as good
hares in the forest as any that have come out of it,
and when I have caught them, I can come back and
look for you."

For many hours he rode up and down the
mountain, but saw nothing, and at last he went back
to the mill. Here he found an old woman sitting,
whom he greeted pleasantly.

"Good morning to you, little mother," he said.

And the old woman answered, "Good morning, my son."

"Tell me, little mother," went on the prince, "where shall I find my hare?"

"My son," replied the old woman, "that was no hare, but a dragon who has led many men hither, and then has eaten them all."

At these words the prince's heart grew heavy, and he cried, "Then my brothers must have come here, and have been eaten!"

"You have guessed right," answered the old woman; "and you should go home at once, before the same fate overtakes you."

"Will you not come with me out of this dreadful place?" said the young man.

"He took me prisoner, too," answered she, "and I cannot shake off his chains."

"Then listen to me," cried the prince. "When the dragon comes back, ask him where he always goes when he leaves here, and what makes him so strong; and when you have coaxed the secret from him, tell me the next time I come."

So the prince went home, and the old woman remained at the mill, and as soon as the dragon returned she said to it, "Where have you been all this time?"

"I have traveled far," it answered.

Then the old woman began to flatter it and, to praise its cleverness, and when she thought she had got it into a good temper, she said, "I have wondered so often where you get your strength from; I do wish you would tell me. I would stoop and kiss the place out of pure love!"

The dragon laughed at this, and answered, "In the hearthstone yonder lies the secret of my strength."

Then the old woman jumped up and kissed the hearth; whereat the dragon laughed the more, and said, "You foolish creature! I was only jesting. It is not in the hearthstone, but in that tall tree that lies the secret of my strength." Then the old woman jumped up again and put her arms round the tree, and kissed it heartily. Loudly laughed the dragon when it saw what she was doing.

"Old fool," it cried, "did you really believe that my strength came from that tree?"

"Where is it then?" asked the old woman, rather crossly, for she did not like being made fun of.

"My strength," replied the dragon, "lies far away; so far that you could never reach it. Far from here is a kingdom, and by its capital city is a lake, and in the lake is a dragon, and inside the dragon is a wild boar, and inside the boar a hare, and inside the hare a pigeon, and inside the pigeon a sparrow, and inside the sparrow is my strength." And when the old woman heard this, she saw it was no use flattering it any longer, for never could she take its strength away.

The following morning, when the dragon had left the mill, the prince came back, and the old woman told him everything that the creature had said. He listened in silence, and then returned to the castle, where he put on a suit of shepherd's clothes, and taking a staff in his hand, he went forth to seek a place as tender of sheep.

For some time he wandered from village to town, till he came to a large city in a distant kingdom, surrounded on three sides by a great lake, which happened to be the very lake in which the dragon lived. As was his custom, he stopped everybody whom he met in the streets that looked likely to want a shepherd and begged them to engage him, but no one needed one. The prince was beginning to lose heart, when a man said that he had better go and ask the emperor, as he was in search of someone to look after his flocks.

When the young man knelt before the emperor,
His Majesty said, "Outside the city walls you will
find a large lake, and by its banks lie the richest
meadows in my kingdom. When you are leading out
your flocks to pasture, they will run straight to these
meadows, and none that have gone there have ever
come back. Take heed, therefore, my son, not to suffer
your sheep to go where they will, but drive them to
any spot that you think best."

With a low bow the prince promised to do his best
to keep the sheep safe. Then he went to the market
place, where he bought two greyhounds, a hawk, and
a set of pipes; after that he took the sheep out to
pasture. The instant the animals caught sight of the
lake, they trotted off as fast as their legs would go to
the green meadows round it. The prince did not try
to stop them; he only placed his hawk on the branch
of a tree, laid his pipes on the grass, and bade the
greyhounds sit still; then he waded into the water
crying as he did so, "Dragon! If you are not a coward,
come out and fight with me!"

And a voice answered from the depths of the lake, "I am waiting for you, O prince." And the dragon reared out of the water, huge and horrible to see.

The prince sprang upon him and they grappled with each other and fought together till the sun was high, and it was noon. Then the dragon gasped, "O prince, let me dip my burning head once into the lake, and I will hurl you up to the sky."

But the prince answered, "Oh ho, my good dragon, do not crow too soon! If the emperor's daughter were only here, and would kiss me on the forehead, I would throw you up higher still!" And suddenly the dragon's hold loosened and it fell back into the lake.

As soon as it was evening, the prince washed away all signs of the fight, took his hawk upon his shoulder, and his pipes under his arm, and with his greyhounds in front and his flock following after him he set out for the city. As they passed through the streets the people stared in wonder, for never before had any flock returned from the lake.

The next morning he rose early and led his sheep

down the road to the lake. This time, however, the emperor sent two men on horseback to ride behind him, with orders to watch without being seen. As soon as the sheep ran toward the meadows, they turned aside up a steep hill, which overhung the lake. When the shepherd reached the place he laid, as before, his pipes on the grass and bade the greyhounds sit beside them, while the hawk he perched on the branch of the tree. Then he waded into the water crying, "Dragon! If you are not a coward, come out and fight with me!"

And the dragon answered, "I am waiting for you, O prince," and it reared out of the water, huge and horrible to see. Again they clasped each other tight and fought till it was noon, and when the sun was at its hottest, the dragon gasped, "O prince, let me dip my burning head once in the lake, and I will hurl you up to the sky."

But the prince answered, "Oh ho, my good dragon, do not crow too soon! If the emperor's daughter were only here, and would kiss me on the forehead, I

would throw you up higher still!" And suddenly the dragon's hold loosened and it fell back into the lake.

As soon as it was evening the prince again collected his sheep and, playing on his pipes, he marched before them into the city. And when he passed through the gates all the people came out of their houses to stare in wonder, because they had once more returned.

Meanwhile the two horsemen had ridden quickly back and told the emperor all. The emperor listened eagerly, then called his daughter to him and repeated it to her. "Tomorrow," he said, when he had finished, "you shall go with the shepherd to the lake, and you shall kiss him on the forehead as he wishes."

But when the princess heard these words, she burst into tears, and sobbed, "Will you really send me, your only child, to that dreadful place, from which most likely I shall never come back?"

"Fear nothing, my little daughter, all will be well. Many shepherds have gone to that lake and none have ever returned; but this one has in these two days fought twice with the dragon and has escaped without a wound. So I hope tomorrow that he will kill the dragon, and deliver this land from the terrible monster that has slain so many of our bravest men for so many years."

Scarcely had the sun begun to peep over the hills next morning, when the princess stood by the shepherd's side, ready to go to the lake. The shepherd was brimming over with joy, but the princess only wept bitterly. "Dry your tears, I implore you," said he. "If you will do what I ask, and when the time comes, run and kiss my forehead, you have nothing to fear."

Merrily the shepherd blew on his pipes as he marched at the head of his flock, only stopping every now and then to comfort the poor weeping princess at his side, "Do not cry so; trust me and fear nothing."

And so they reached the lake.

In an instant the sheep were scattered all over the meadows, and the prince placed his hawk on the tree, and his pipes on the grass, while he bade his

greyhounds lie beside them. Then he waded into the water, calling, "Dragon! If you are not a coward, come forth, and let us have one more fight together."

And the dragon answered, "I am waiting for you, O prince," and reared out of the water, huge and horrible to see. Swiftly it drew near to the bank, and the prince sprang to meet him, and they grasped each other and fought till it was noon. And when the sun was at its hottest, the dragon cried, "O prince, let me dip my burning head in the lake, and I will hurl you to the sky."

But the prince answered, "Oh ho, my good dragon, do not crow too soon! If the emperor's daughter were only here, and she would kiss my forehead, I would throw you higher still."

Hardly had he spoken these words, when the princess, who had been listening all along, ran up to him and kissed him on the forehead. Then the prince swung the dragon straight up into the clouds, and when it fell back to the earth again, it broke into a thousand pieces. Out of the pieces there sprang a wild boar and it galloped away, but the prince called his hounds to give chase, and they caught the boar and tore it to bits. Out of the pieces there sprang a hare, and in a moment the greyhounds were after it, and they caught it and killed it; and out of the hare there came a pigeon. Quickly the prince let loose his hawk, which soared into the air, then swooped upon the bird and brought it to his master.

The prince cut open its body and found the sparrow inside, just as the old woman had said.

"Now," cried the prince, holding the sparrow in his hand, "now you shall tell me where I can find my brothers."

"Do not hurt me," answered the sparrow, "and I will tell you with all my heart. Behind your father's castle stands a mill, and in the mill are three slender twigs. Cut off these twigs and strike their roots with them, and the iron door of a cellar will open. In the cellar you will find as many people, young and old, women and children, as would fill a kingdom, and among them are your brothers."

By this time twilight had fallen, so the prince washed in the lake, took the hawk on his shoulder and the pipes under his arm, and with his greyhounds before him and his flock behind him, marched gaily into the town, the princess following them all, still trembling with fright. And so they passed through the streets, thronged with a wondering crowd, till they reached the castle.

Unknown to anyone, the emperor had stolen out on horseback, and had hidden on the hill, where he could see all that happened. When all was over, and the power of the dragon was broken forever, he rode quickly back to the castle, and was ready to receive the prince with open arms, and to promise him his daughter as a wife. The wedding took place with great splendor, and for a whole week the town was hung with colored lamps, and tables were spread in the hall of the castle for all who chose to come and eat. And when the feast was over, the prince told the emperor and the people who he really was, and everyone rejoiced still more, and preparations were made for the prince and princess to return to their own kingdom, for the prince was impatient to set free his brothers.

The first thing he did when he reached his native country was to hasten to the mill, where he found the three twigs just as the sparrow had told him. The moment that he struck their roots the iron door flew open, and from the cellar a countless multitude of men and women streamed forth. He bade them go one by one wheresoever they would, while he waited patiently by the door till his brothers passed through. How delighted they all were to meet again, and to hear all that the prince had done to deliver them from

their fate. And they returned home and served him all
the days of their lives, for they said that only he was
fit to be king.

The Ogre of Rashomon

From *Japanese Fairy Tales* by Yei Theodora Ozaki

LONG AGO in Kyoto, the people of the city were terrified by, it was said, a dreadful ogre who haunted the Gate of Rashomon at twilight and seized whoever passed by. It was whispered that the ogre was a horrible cannibal, who not only killed the unhappy victims but ate them also. Now everybody in the town and neighborhood was in great fear, and no one dared venture out after sunset near the Gate of Rashomon for fear of the terrible stories.

Five valiant knights came traveling through the province, and one night, as the five sat at a feast, toasting each other's healths and exploits, the first knight, Hojo, said to the others: "Have you heard the rumors about the ogre at the Gate of Rashomon?"

The second knight, Watanabe, answered him, saying, "Do not talk such nonsense! There is no longer such thing as ogres."

"Then go there yourself and find out whether it is true or not," said Hojo.

Watanabe, the second knight, could not bear the thought that his companion should believe he was afraid, so he at once got ready to go—he buckled on his long sword and put on a coat of armor, and tied on his large helmet. When he was ready to start he said to the others, "Give me something so that I can prove I have been there!" Then one of the men got a roll of writing paper and his box of Indian ink and brushes, and the four comrades wrote their names on a piece of paper. "I will take this," said Watanabe, "and put it on the Gate of Rashomon, so tomorrow morning you will all go and look at it. I may be able to catch an ogre or two by then!" and he mounted his horse and rode off gallantly.

It was a moonless and stormy night, but Watanabe sped on and at last he reached the Gate of Rashomon. Peer as he might through the darkness he could see no sign of an ogre. "It is just as I thought," said Watanabe to himself; "there are certainly no ogres here; it is only an old woman's story. I will stick this paper on the gate so that the others can see I have been here when they come tomorrow, and then I will make my way home and laugh at them all." He fastened the piece of paper, signed by all his four companions, on the gate, and then turned his horse's head toward home.

As he did so, his helmet was seized from the back. "Who are you?" cried Watanabe fearlessly. He then put out his hand and groped around to find out who or what it was that held him by the helmet. As he did so he touched something that felt like an arm—it was covered with hair and was as big as a tree trunk!

Watanabe knew at once that this was the arm of an ogre, so he drew his sword and cut at it fiercely. There was a loud yell of pain, and then the ogre dashed in front of the warrior. Watanabe's eyes grew large with wonder, for he saw that the ogre was taller than the great gate, his eyes were flashing like mirrors in the sunlight, and his huge mouth was wide open, and as the monster breathed, flames of fire shot out of his mouth.

Watanabe never flinched. He attacked the ogre with all his strength, and thus they fought face to face for a long time. At last the ogre, finding that he could neither frighten nor beat Watanabe and that he might himself be beaten, took to flight. But Watanabe, determined not to let the monster escape, put spurs to his horse and gave chase. But though the knight rode very fast the ogre ran faster, and to his disappointment he found himself unable to overtake the monster, who was gradually lost to sight.

Watanabe returned to the gate where the fierce fight had taken place, and got down from his horse. As he did so he stumbled upon something lying on the ground. Stooping to pick it up he found that it was one of the ogre's huge arms, which he must have slashed off in the fight. His joy was great at having secured such a prize, for this was the best of all proofs of his adventure with the ogre. So he took it up and carried it home as a trophy of his victory.

When he got back, he showed the arm to his comrades, who one and all called him the hero of their band and gave him a great feast. His wonderful deed was soon heard abroad in Kyoto, and people from far and near came to see the ogre's arm.

Watanabe now began to grow uneasy as to how he should keep the arm in safety, for he knew that the ogre to whom it belonged was still alive. He felt sure that one day or other, as soon as the ogre got over his scare, he would come to try to get his arm back again. Watanabe therefore had a box made of the strongest wood and banded with iron. In this he placed the arm, and then he sealed down the heavy lid, refusing to open it for anyone. He kept the box in his own room and took charge of it himself, never allowing it out of his sight.

Now one night he heard someone knocking at the porch, asking for admittance. When the servant went to the door to see who it was, there was only an old woman, very respectable in appearance. On being asked who she was and what was her business, the old woman replied with a smile that she had been nurse to the master of the house when he was a little baby. If the lord of the house were at home she begged to be allowed to see him.

The servant left the old woman at the door and went to tell his master that his old nurse had come to see him. Watanabe thought it strange that she should come at that time of night, but at the thought of his old nurse, who had been like a foster mother to him and whom he had not seen for a long time, a very tender feeling sprang up for her in his heart. He ordered the servant to show her in.

The old woman was ushered into the room, and after the customary bows and greetings were over, she said, "Master, the report of your brave fight with the ogre at the Gate of Rashomon is so widely known that even your poor old nurse has heard of it. I am very proud to think that my master was so brave as to dare to cut off an ogre's arm. Before I die it is the great wish of my life to see this arm."

"No," said Watanabe, "I am sorry, but I cannot

grant your request. Ogres are very revengeful creatures, and if I open the box there is no telling but that he may suddenly appear and carry off his arm."

The woman pleaded and pleaded, but Watanabe still refused.

Then the old woman said, "Do you suspect me of being a spy sent by the ogre?"

"No, of course I do not suspect you of being the ogre's spy, for you are my old nurse," Watanabe answered her.

"Then you cannot refuse to show me the arm any longer," entreated the old woman; "for it is the great wish of my heart to see for once in my life the arm of an ogre!"

Watanabe could not hold out in his refusal any longer, so he gave in at last. And he led the way to his own room, the old woman following.

When they were both in the room Watanabe shut the door carefully, and then going toward a big box that stood in a corner of the room, he took off the heavy lid and called the old woman to come near.

"What is it like? Let me have a good look at it," said the old nurse, with a joyful face.

She came nearer and nearer, as if she were afraid, till she stood right against the box. Suddenly she plunged her hand into the box and seized the arm, crying with a fearful voice that made the room shake:

"Oh, joy is me! I have got my arm back at last!" And from the body of a frail old woman she was suddenly transformed into the towering figure of the frightful ogre!

Watanabe sprang back and was unable to move for a moment, so great was his astonishment; but recognizing the ogre who had attacked him at the Gate of Rashomon, he determined with his usual courage to put an end to him this time. He seized his sword, drew it out of its sheath in a flash, and tried to cut the ogre down.

So quick was Watanabe that the creature had a narrow escape. But the ogre sprang up to the ceiling and, bursting through the roof, disappeared in the mist and clouds.

In this way the ogre escaped with his arm. The knight gnashed his teeth with disappointment, but that was all he could do. He waited in patience for another opportunity to dispatch the ogre. But the latter was afraid of Watanabe's great strength and daring, and never troubled the city of Kyoto again. So once more the people of the city were able to go out without fear even at night time, and the brave deeds of Watanabe have never been forgotten!

Mr Miacca

From *English Fairy Tales* by Joseph Jacobs

TOMMY GRIMES was sometimes good, and sometimes bad; and when he was bad, he was very bad. Now his mother used to say to him, "Tommy, Tommy, be good, and don't go out into the street, or else Mr Miacca will take you." But one day when he was bad he went out into the street and, sure enough, Mr Miacca did catch him and popped him into a bag upside down, and took him off to his house.

Mr Miacca pulled Tommy out of the bag and set him down, and felt his arms and legs.

"You're rather tough," says he, "but you're all I've got for supper, and you'll not taste bad boiled. But body o' me, I've forgot the herbs, and it's bitter you'll taste without herbs." And he called Mrs Miacca.

Mrs Miacca came out of another room and said, "What d'ye want, my dear?"

"Oh, here's a little boy for supper," said Mr Miacca, "and I've forgot the herbs. Mind him, while I go for them."

"All right, my love," says Mrs Miacca, and off her husband goes.

Then Tommy Grimes said to Mrs Miacca: "Does Mr Miacca always have little boys for supper?"

"Mostly, my dear," said Mrs Miacca, "if little boys are bad enough, and get in his way."

"And don't you have anything else but boy-meat? No dessert?" asked Tommy.

"Ah, I loves dessert," says Mrs Miacca. "But it's not often the likes of me gets dessert."

"Why, my mother is making a dessert this very day," said Tommy Grimes, "and I am sure she'd give you some, if I ask her. Shall I run and get some?"

"Now, that's a thoughtful boy," said Mrs Miacca, "only don't be long and be back for supper."

So off Tommy runs, and right glad he was to get off so easily; and for many a long day he was as good as good could be, and never went out into the street. But he couldn't always be good; and one day he went out into the street, and as luck would have it, he hadn't scarcely gone out when Mr Miacca grabbed him up, popped him in his bag, and took him home.

When he got him there, Mr Miacca dropped him out; and when he saw him, he said: "Ah, you're the youngster what served me and my wife that shabby trick, leaving us without any supper. Well, you shan't do it again. I'll watch over you myself. Here, get under the sofa, and I'll sit on it and wait for the pot to boil for you."

So poor Tommy Grimes had to creep under the sofa, and Mr Miacca sat on it and waited for the pot to boil. And they waited, and they waited, but still the pot didn't boil, till at last Mr Miacca got tired of waiting, and he said, "Here, you under there, I'm not going to wait any longer; put out your leg, and I'll stop your giving us the slip."

So Tommy put out a leg, and Mr Miacca chopped it off, and popped it in the pot.

Suddenly he called for his wife, but nobody answered. So he went into the next room to look for Mrs Miacca, and while he was there, Tommy crept out from under the sofa and ran out of the door, for it was a leg of the sofa that he had put out.

So Tommy Grimes ran home, and he never went out into the street again until he was old enough to go alone.

The Gifts of the Little People

The Brothers Grimm

A TAILOR AND A GOLDSMITH were journeying together when one evening, just as the sun had sunk behind the mountains, they heard the sound of distant music. It had a strange sound, but was so pleasing that they forgot their weariness and walked speedily ahead. The moon had already risen when they arrived at a hill, upon which they viewed a large number of small men and women, who were holding hands and dancing around and cheerfully singing with the greatest pleasure and happiness. That was the music that the wanderers had heard.

An old man, somewhat larger than the others, sat in their midst. He wore a brightly colored jacket, and his ice-gray beard hung down over his chest. Filled with amazement, the two wanderers stopped and watched the dance. The old man motioned to them that they too should join in, and the little people voluntarily opened their circle.

The goldsmith, who had a hump on his back but was bold rather than self-conscious, stepped right up. The tailor was at first a little shy and held back, but as soon as he saw what fun it was, he too took heart and joined in.

They closed the circle again, and the little people sang and danced wildly. However, the old man took a broad knife that had been hanging from his belt, sharpened it, and looked at the strangers. They were frightened, but they did not have to worry for long. The old man grabbed the goldsmith and with the greatest speed smoothly shaved off his beard and the hair from his head. Then the same thing happened to the tailor. Their fear disappeared when the old man

patted them friendly on their shoulders, as if to say
that they had done well by letting it all happen
without resisting. With his finger he pointed toward a
pile of coal that lay nearby, and indicated to them
through gestures that they should fill their pockets
with it. They both obeyed, although they did not
know of what use the coal would be to them. Then
they went on their way to seek out a place to spend
the night.

They had just arrived in a valley when the bell from a neighboring monastery struck twelve. The distant sound of the little people's singing ceased instantly. The two wanderers found shelter. Lying on beds of straw, they covered themselves with their jackets. They were so tired that they forgot to take the coal out of their pockets first.

They were awakened earlier than normal by a heavy weight pressing down on their limbs. They reached into their pockets, and could hardly believe their eyes when they saw that they were not filled with coal, but with pure gold. Further, their hair and their beards had also been fully restored.

Now they were rich. However, the goldsmith had twice as much as the tailor, because—true to his greedy nature—he had filled his pockets better. However much a greedy person has, he always wants more, so the goldsmith proposed to the tailor that they stay there another day, in order to be able to gain even more wealth from the old man on the mountain that evening.

The tailor did not want to do this, and said, "I have enough and am satisfied. I am going to become a master, marry my sweetheart, and be a happy man." However, to please the goldsmith, he agreed to stay one more day.

That evening the goldsmith hung several pockets over his shoulders in order to be able to carry everything, and set off for the hill. As had happened the night before, he found the little people dancing and singing. The old man shaved him smooth once again, and indicated that he should take some coal. Without hesitating he packed away as much as his pockets would hold, and then happily returned home. Covering himself with his jacket he said, "I can bear it, if the gold presses down on me." With the sweet idea that he would awaken tomorrow as a very rich man, he fell asleep.

When he opened his eyes, he got up quickly in order to examine his pockets. How astounded he was, that he pulled out nothing but black coal, however often he reached inside. 'Anyway, I still have the gold

from the night before,' he thought, and reached for it. Horrified, he saw that it too had turned back into coal. He struck himself on the forehead with his grimy hand, and felt that his entire head was as bald and smooth as his beardless chin.

Nor was that the end of his misfortune. He suddenly noticed that in addition to the hump on his back, a second one, of the same size, had grown on his chest. Now he recognized the punishment for his greed and began to cry aloud.

The good tailor, who had been awakened by all this, consoled the unhappy man as best he could, saying: "You were my traveling companion, and you can stay with me now and live from my treasure."

He kept his word, but the poor goldsmith had to bear two humps and cover his bald head with a cap as long as he lived.

Tritill, Litill, and the Birds

From Andrew Lang's *Crimson Fairy Book*

ONCE UPON A TIME there lived a princess who was so beautiful and so good that everybody loved her. Her father almost died of grief when, one day, she disappeared, and though the whole kingdom was searched, she could not be found in any corner of it. In despair, the king ordered that whoever could find her should have her for his wife. This made the young men search afresh, but they were no more successful than before, and returned sorrowfully to their homes.

Now there dwelled, not far from the palace, a man

and a wife who had three sons. The two eldest were allowed by their parents to do just as they liked, but the youngest was always obliged to give way to his brothers. When they were all grown up, the eldest told his father that he meant to go away and see the world. The old people were very unhappy, but they said nothing, and began to prepare for his travels. When everything was ready, he bade them farewell.

He walked for some miles through a wood and came out on a bare hillside. Here he sat down to rest and, pulling out his wallet, prepared to eat his dinner. He had only eaten a few mouthfuls when an old man, badly dressed, passed by and, seeing the food, asked if the young man could not spare him a little.

"Not I, indeed!" answered he. "Why I have scarcely enough for myself. If you want food you must earn it."

And the beggar went on.

After the young man had finished his dinner he walked on for several hours, till he reached a second hill, where he threw himself down on the grass, and took some bread and milk from his wallet. While he was eating and drinking, there came by an old man, yet more wretched than the first, and begged for a few mouthfuls. But instead of food he only got hard words, and limped sadly away.

Toward evening the young man reached an open space in the wood, and by this time he thought he would like some supper. The birds saw the food, and flew round his head hoping for some crumbs, but he threw stones at them and frightened them off. Then he began to wonder where he should sleep. Not where he was, for that was bare and cold, and though he had walked a long way and was tired, he dragged himself up and went on seeking for a shelter.

At length he saw a deep sort of hole or cave under a great rock, and as it seemed quite empty, he went in and lay down in a corner. About midnight he was awakened by a noise and, peeping out, he beheld a terrible ogress approaching. He implored her not to hurt him, but to let him stay there for the rest of the night, to which she consented, on condition that he should spend the next day in doing any task which she might choose to set him. To this the young man agreed, and turned over and went to sleep again.

In the morning, the ogress bade him sweep the dust out of the cave, and to have it clean before her return in the evening, otherwise it would be the worse for him. Then she left.

The young man began to clean the floor of the cave, but try as he would to move it, the dirt still stuck to its place. He soon gave up the task and sat sulkily in the corner, wondering what punishment the ogress would find for him and why she had set him to do such an impossible thing.

He had not long to wait, after the ogress came home, before he knew what his punishment was to be! She just gave one look at the floor of the cave, then dealt him a blow on the head that cracked his skull, and there was an end of him.

Meanwhile his next brother grew tired of staying at home and let his parents have no rest till they had consented that he also should go out to see the world. He also met the two old beggars, who prayed for a little of his bread and milk, but this young man had never been taught to help other people, so he turned a deaf ear and finished his dinner.

By and by he, too, came to the cave, and was bidden by the ogress to clean the floor, but he was no more successful than his brother, and his fate was the same.

Anyone would have thought that when the old people had only one son left that at least they would have been kind to him, even if they did not love him. But for some reason they could hardly bear the sight of him, though he tried much harder to make them comfortable than his brothers had ever done. So when he asked their leave to go out into the world they gave it at once, and seemed quite glad to be rid of him.

Besides the pleasure of seeing the world, the youth was very anxious to discover what had become of his brothers, and he determined to trace, as far as he could, the way that they must have gone. He followed the road that led from his father's cottage to the hill, where he sat down to rest, saying to himself, "I am sure my brothers must have stopped here, and I will do the same."

He was hungry as well as tired, and took out some food. He was just going to begin to eat when the old man appeared. The young man at once broke off some of the bread, begging the old man to sit down beside him, and treating him as if he was an old friend. At last the stranger rose, and said to him, "If ever you are in trouble call me, and I will help you. My name is Tritill." Then he vanished.

At the next hill he met with the second old man, and to him also he gave food and drink. And when this old man had finished he said, like the first, "If you ever want help in the smallest thing call to me. My name is Litill."

The young man walked on till he reached the open space in the wood, where he stopped for dinner. In a moment all the birds in the world seemed to be flying round his head, and he crumbled some of his bread for them and watched them dart down to pick it up. When they had cleared off every crumb, the largest bird with the brightest plumage said to him, "If you are in trouble and need help say, 'My birds, come to me!' and we will come." Then they flew away.

Toward evening the young man reached the cave

where his brothers had met their deaths, and, like them, he thought it would be a good place to sleep in. Looking round, he saw some pieces of the dead men's clothes and of their bones. The sight made him shiver, but he would not move away, and resolved to await the return of the ogress, for such he knew she must be.

Very soon she came striding in, and he asked politely if she would give him a night's lodging. She answered as before, that he might stay on condition that he should do any work that she might set him to next morning. So the bargain being concluded, the young man curled himself up in his corner and went to sleep.

The dirt lay thicker than ever on the floor of the cave when the young man took the shovel and began his work. He could not clear it any more than his brothers had done, and at last the shovel itself stuck in the earth so that he could not pull it out. The youth stared at it in despair, then the old beggar's words flashed into his mind, and he cried, "Tritill,

Tritill, come and help me!"

And Tritill stood beside him and asked what he wanted. The youth told him all his story, and when he had finished, the old man said: "Shovel do your duty," and it danced about the cave till, in a short time, there was not a speck of dust left on the floor. As soon as it was quite clean Tritill went his way.

With a light heart the young man awaited the return of the ogress. When she came in she looked carefully round, and then said to him, "You did not do that quite alone. However, as the floor is clean I will leave your head on."

The following morning the ogress told the young man that he must take all the feathers out of her pillows and spread them to dry in the sun. But if one feather was missing when she came back at night his head should pay for it.

The young man fetched the pillows, and shook out all the feathers, and oh, what quantities of them there were! Suddenly a breeze sprang up, and in a moment the feathers were dancing high in the air. At first the youth tried to collect them again, but he soon found that it was no use, and he cried in despair, "Tritill, Litill, and my birds, come and help me!"

He had hardly said the words when there they all were; and when the birds had brought all the feathers back again, Tritill and Litill and he put them away in the pillows, as the ogress had bidden him. But one feather they kept out, and told the young man that if the ogress missed it he was to thrust it up her nose. Then they all vanished, Tritill, Litill, and the birds.

As soon as the ogress returned home she flung herself on the bed and the whole cave quivered under her. The pillows were soft and full instead of being empty, which surprised her, but that did not content her. The ogress got up, shook out all of the pillowcases one by one, and began to count the feathers in each. "If one is missing I will have your head," said the ogress.

And at that the young man drew the feather from his pocket and thrust it up her nose, crying, "If you want your feather, here it is."

"You did not sort those feathers alone," answered the ogress calmly; "however, I will let that pass."

That night the young man slept soundly, and in the morning the ogress told him that his work that day

would be to slay one of her great oxen, to cook its
heart, and to make drinking cups of its horns, before
she returned home. "There are fifty oxen," added she,
"and you must guess which of the herd I want killed.
If you guess right, tomorrow you shall be free to go
where you will, and you shall choose three things as a
reward for your service. But if you slay the wrong ox
your head shall pay for it."

When he was left alone, the young man stood
thinking for a little. Then he called, "Tritill, Litill,
come to my help!"

In a moment he saw them, far away, driving the
biggest ox the youth had ever seen. When they drew
near, Tritill killed it, Litill took out its heart for the
young man to cook, and they both began to quickly
turn the horns into drinking cups. The old men
warned the youth that he must ask the ogress for the
chest which stood at the foot of her bed, for whatever
lay on the top of the bed, and for what lay under the
side of the cave. The young man thanked them for
their counsel, and Tritill and Litill then took leave of

him, saying that for the present he would need them
no more.

Scarcely had they disappeared when the ogress
came back, and found everything ready just as she had
ordered. Before she sat down to eat the heart she
turned to the young man, and said, "You did not do
that all alone, my friend; but, nevertheless, I will keep
my word, and tomorrow you shall go your way." So
they went to bed and slept till dawn.

When the sun rose the ogress awoke the young
man, and called to him to choose any three things out
of her house.

"I choose," answered he, "the chest which stands at
the foot of your bed; whatever lies on the top of the
bed, and whatever is under the side of the cave."

"You did not choose those things by yourself, my
friend," said the ogress, "but what I have promised,
that will I do."

And then she gave him his reward.

The thing that lay on the top of the bed turned
out to be the lost princess. The chest which stood at

the foot of the bed proved to be full of gold and precious stones; and what was under the side of the cave he found to be a great ship, with oars and sails, that went of itself as well on land as in the water. "You are the luckiest man that ever was born," said the ogress as she went out of the cave as usual.

With much difficulty the youth put the heavy chest on his shoulders and carried it on board the ship, the princess walking by his side. Then he took the helm and steered the vessel back to her father's kingdom. The king's joy at receiving back his lost daughter was so great that he almost fainted, but when he recovered himself he made the young man tell him how everything had really happened. "You

have found her, and therefore you shall marry her,"
said the king; and so it was done. And this is the end
of the story.

The Sprightly Tailor

From *Celtic Fairy Tales* by Joseph Jacobs

A SPRIGHTLY TAILOR was employed by the great Macdonald, in his castle at Saddell, in order to make the laird a pair of trews, used in olden time. And trews were a vest and breeches sewn into one garment and ornamented with fringes —they were very comfortable, and suitable to be worn in walking or dancing. And Macdonald had said to the tailor, that if he would make the trews by night in the church, he would get a handsome reward. For it was thought that the old ruined church was haunted, and that fearsome things were to be seen there at night.

The tailor was well aware of this; but he was a sprightly man, and when the laird dared him to make the trews by night in the church, the tailor was not to be daunted, but took it in hand to gain the prize. So, when night came, away he went up the glen, about half a mile distance from the castle, till he came to the old church. Then he chose him a nice gravestone for a seat and he lighted his candle, and put on his thimble, and set to work at the trews; plying his needle nimbly, and thinking about the reward that the laird would have to give him.

For some time he got on pretty well, until he felt the floor all of a tremble under his feet; and looking about him, but keeping his fingers at work, he saw the appearance of a great human head rising up through the stone floor of the church. And when the head had risen above the surface, there came from it a great, great voice. And the voice said, "Do you see this great head of mine?"

"I see that, but I'll sew this!" replied the sprightly tailor, and he stitched away at the trews.

Then the head rose higher up through the floor, until its neck appeared. And when its neck was shown, the thundering voice came again and said to the tailor, "Do you see this great neck of mine?"

"I see that, but I'll sew this!" said the sprightly tailor; and he stitched away at his trews.

Then the head and neck rose higher still, until the

great shoulders and chest were shown above the ground. And again the mighty voice thundered, "Do you see this great chest of mine?"

And again the sprightly tailor replied, "I see that, but I'll sew this!" and stitched away at his trews.

And still it kept rising through the floor, until it shook a great pair of arms in the tailor's face, and said, "Do you see these great arms of mine?"

"I see those, but I'll sew this!" answered the tailor, and he stitched hard at his trews, for he knew that he had no time to lose.

The sprightly tailor was taking the long stitches, when he saw it gradually rising and rising through the floor, until it lifted out a great leg, and stamping with it upon the floor, said in a roaring voice, "Do you see this great leg of mine?"

"Aye, aye. I see that, but I'll sew this!" cried the tailor, and his fingers flew with the needle, and he took such long stitches, that he was just coming to the

end of the trews, when it was taking up its other leg.
But before it could pull it out of the floor, the
sprightly tailor had finished his task; and, blowing out
his candle and springing from off his gravestone, he
buckled up, and ran out of the church with the trews
under his arm. Then the fearsome thing gave a loud
roar, and stamped both its feet upon the floor, and
out of the church it went after the sprightly tailor.

Down the glen they ran, faster than the stream
when the flood rides it, but the tailor had got the
start and a nimble pair of legs, and he did not choose
to lose the laird's reward. And though the thing
roared to him to stop, yet the sprightly tailor was not
the man to be beholden to a monster. So he held his
trews tight, and let no darkness grow under his feet,
until he had reached Saddell Castle. He had no
sooner got inside the gate and shut it, than the
apparition came up to it, and enraged at losing its
prize, struck the wall above the gate, and left there the
mark of its five great fingers. You may see them
plainly to this day, if you'll only peer close enough.

But the sprightly tailor gained his reward. For Macdonald paid him handsomely for the trews, and never discovered that a few of the stitches were somewhat long.

DOOM AND DEATH

The Goblin of Adachigahara

From *Japanese Fairy Tales* by Yei Theodora Ozaki

LONG, LONG AGO there was a large plain called Adachigahara in Japan. This place was said to be haunted by a cannibal goblin who took the form of an old woman. From time to time many travelers disappeared and were never heard of more. The old women round the charcoal braziers in the evenings, and the girls washing the household rice at the wells in the mornings, whispered dreadful stories of how the missing folk had been lured to the goblin's cottage and devoured, for the goblin lived only on human flesh. No one dared to venture near the haunted spot after sunset, and all those who could, avoided it in the daytime, and travelers were warned to avoid the dreaded place.

One day as the sun was setting, a priest came to the plain. His robe showed that he was a Buddhist pilgrim walking from shrine to shrine to pray for some blessing or to crave for forgiveness of sins. He had apparently lost his way, and as it was late he met no one who could show him the road or warn him of the haunted spot.

He had walked the whole day and was now very tired and hungry. The evenings were chilly, for it was late autumn, and he began to feel anxious to find some house where he could obtain a night's lodging. But he found himself lost in the midst of the large plain, and looked about in vain for some sign of human dwelling.

At last, after wandering about for some hours, he saw a clump of trees in the distance, and through the trees he caught sight of the glimmer of a single ray of light. He exclaimed with joy, "Oh, surely that is some

DOOM AND DEATH

The Goblin of Adachigahara

cottage where I can get a night's lodging!"

Keeping the light before his eyes he dragged his weary, aching feet as quickly as he could toward the spot, and soon came to a miserable-looking little cottage. As he drew near he saw that it was in a tumble-down condition, the bamboo fence was broken and weeds and grass pushed their way through the gaps. The paper screens that serve as windows and doors in Japan were full of holes, and the posts of the house were bent with age and seemed scarcely able to support the old thatched roof. The hut was open, and by the light of an old lantern an old woman sat industriously spinning.

The pilgrim called to her across the bamboo fence and said, "Good evening, old woman—I am a traveler! Please excuse me, but I have lost my way and do not know what to do, for I have nowhere to rest tonight. I beg you to be good enough to let me spend the night under your roof."

The old woman, as soon as she heard herself spoken to, stopped spinning, rose from her seat and approached the intruder.

"I am very sorry for you. You must indeed be distressed to have lost your way in such a spot so late at night. But unfortunately I cannot put you up, for I have no bed to offer you, and no accommodation whatsoever for a guest in this poor lonely place!"

"Oh, that does not matter," said the priest, "all I

want is a shelter under some roof for the night, and if you will be good enough just to let me lie on the kitchen floor I shall be grateful. I am too tired to walk further tonight, so I hope you will not refuse me, otherwise I shall have to sleep out on the cold plain." And in this way he pressed the old woman to let him stay.

She seemed very reluctant, but at last she said, "Very well, I will let you stay here. I can offer you a very poor welcome only, but come in now and I will make a fire, for the night is cold."

The pilgrim was only too glad to do as he was told. He took off his sandals and entered the hut. The old woman then brought some sticks of wood and lit the fire, and bade her guest draw near and warm himself.

"You must be hungry after your long walk," said the old woman. "I will go and cook some supper for you." She then went to the kitchen to cook some rice.

After the priest had finished his supper the old woman sat down by the fireplace, and they talked together for a long time. The pilgrim thought to himself that he had been very lucky to come across such a kind, hospitable old woman. At last the wood gave out, and as the fire died slowly down he began to shiver with cold just as he had done when he arrived.

"I see you are cold," said the old woman; "I will go out and gather some wood, for we have used it all. You must stay here and take care of the house."

"No, no," said the pilgrim, "let me go instead, for you are old, and I cannot think of letting you go out to get wood for me on this cold night!"

The old woman shook her head and said, "You must stay quietly here, for you are my guest." Then she left him and went out.

In a minute she came back and said, "You must sit where you are and not move, and whatever happens don't go near or look into the back room. Now mind what I tell you!"

"If you tell me not to go near the back room, of course I won't," said the priest, rather bewildered.

The old woman then went out again and the priest

was left alone. The fire had died out and the only light in the hut was that of a dim lantern. For the first time that night he began to feel that he was in a weird place, and the old woman's words, "Whatever you do don't peep into the back room," aroused his curiosity and his fear.

What hidden thing could be in that room that she did not wish him to see? For some time the remembrance of his promise to the old woman kept him still, but at last he could no longer resist his curiosity to peep into the forbidden place.

He got up and began to move slowly toward the back room. Then the thought that the old woman would be very angry with him if he disobeyed her made him come back to his place by the fireside.

As the minutes went slowly by and the old woman did not return, he began to feel more and more frightened, and to wonder what dreadful secret was in the room behind him. He must find out.

"She will not know that I have looked unless I tell her. I will just have a peep before she comes back."

With these words he got up on his feet (for he had been sitting all this time in Japanese fashion with his feet under him) and stealthily crept toward the forbidden spot. With trembling hands he pushed back the sliding door and looked in. What he saw froze the blood in his veins. The room was full of dead men's bones and the walls were splashed and the floor was covered with human blood. In one corner skull upon skull rose to the ceiling, in another was a heap of arm bones, in another a heap of leg bones. The sickening smell made him faint. He fell backward with horror, and for some time lay in a heap with fright on the floor, a pitiful sight. He trembled all over and his teeth chattered, and he could hardly crawl away from the dreadful spot.

"How horrible!" he cried out. "What awful den have I come to on my travels? May Buddha help me or I am lost. Is it possible that that kind old woman is really the cannibal goblin? When she comes back she will show herself in her true character and eat me up in one mouthful!"

Doom and Death

With these words his strength came back to him and, snatching up his staff, he rushed out of the house as fast as his legs could carry him. Out into the night he ran, his one thought to get as far as he could from the goblin's haunt. He had not gone very far when he heard steps behind him and a voice crying, "Stop! Stop!"

He ran on, doubling his speed, pretending not to hear. As he ran he heard the steps behind him come nearer and nearer, and at last he recognized the old woman's voice which grew louder and louder as she came nearer. "Stop! Stop, you wicked man! Why did you look into the forbidden room?"

The priest quite forgot how tired he was and his feet flew over the ground faster than ever. Fear gave him strength, for he knew that if the goblin caught him he would soon be one of her victims. With all his heart he repeated the prayer to Buddha: "Namu Amida Butsu, Namu Amida Butsu."

And after him rushed the dreadful old hag, her hair flying in the wind, and her face changing with rage into the demon that she was. In her hand she carried a large, bloodstained knife, and she still shrieked after him, "Stop! Stop!"

At last, when the priest felt he could run no more, the dawn broke, and with the darkness of night the goblin vanished and he was safe. The priest now knew that he had met the Goblin of Adachigahara, the story of whom he had often heard but never believed to be true. He felt that he owed his wonderful escape to the protection of Buddha, to whom he had prayed for help, so he took out his rosary and, bowing his head as the sun rose, he said his prayers and made his thanksgiving earnestly. He then set forward for another part of the country, only too glad to leave the haunted plain behind him.

The Red Shoes

By Hans Christian Andersen

Once upon a time there was a little girl, pretty and dainty. But she was extremely poor—so poor that in summertime she was obliged to go barefooted because she had no sandals, and in winter she had to wear large wooden shoes, making her little toes go quite red.

In the middle of the village lived an old shoemaker's wife; she sat down and made, as well as she could, a pair of little shoes out of some old pieces of red cloth. They were clumsy, but she meant well, for they were intended for the little girl, whose name was Karen.

Karen received the shoes and wore them for the first time on the day of her mother's funeral. They were certainly not suitable for mourning; but she had no others, so she put her bare feet into them and walked behind the humble coffin.

Just then a large carriage came by, and in it sat an old lady; she looked at the little girl, and taking pity on her, said to the clergyman, "Look here, if you will give me the little girl, I will take care of her."

Karen believed that this was all on account of the red shoes, but the old lady thought them hideous, so they were burned. Karen was dressed very neatly and cleanly; she was taught to read and to sew, and people said that she was pretty. But the mirror told her, "You are more than pretty—you are beautiful."

One day the queen was traveling through that part of the country and had her little daughter, who was a princess, with her. All the people, amongst them Karen too, streamed toward the castle, where the little princess, in fine white clothes, stood before the

window and allowed herself to be stared at. She wore
neither a train nor a golden crown, but beautiful, red
Morocco shoes; they were indeed much finer than
those that the shoemaker's wife had sewn for little
Karen. There is really nothing in the world that can
be compared to red shoes!

Karen was now old enough to have a special
ceremony at church called confirmation; for
this important occasion she received some
new clothes and she was also to have new
shoes. The rich shoemaker in the town took
the measure of her little foot in his own
room, in which there stood great glass cases
full of pretty shoes and white slippers. It all
looked very lovely, but the old lady could
not see very well, and therefore did not get
much pleasure out of it. Amongst the shoes
stood a pair of red ones, like those which the
princess had worn. The shoemaker said that
they had been made for a count's daughter, but
that they had not fitted her.

"I suppose they are of patent leather?" asked the old lady. "They shine so."

"Yes, they do shine," said Karen. They fitted her, and were bought. But the old lady knew nothing of them being red, for she would never have allowed Karen to be confirmed in bright, bold red shoes, as she was now to be.

Everybody looked at her feet, and the whole of the way from the church door to the choir it seemed to Karen as if even the ancient figures on the monuments, in their stiff collars and long black robes, had their eyes fixed on her red shoes. It was only of these that she thought when the clergyman laid his hand upon her head and spoke of the holy baptism, of the promise to God, and told her that she was now to be a grown-up

Christian. The organ pealed forth solemnly, and the sweet children's voices mingled with that of their old leader; but Karen thought only of her red shoes.

In the afternoon the old lady heard from everybody that Karen had worn red shoes. She said that it was a shocking thing to do, that it was very improper, and that Karen was always to go to church in future in black shoes, even if they were old.

On the following Sunday there was Communion at Mass. Karen looked first at the black shoes, then at the red ones—looked at the red ones again, and put them on.

The sun was shining gloriously, so Karen and the old lady went along the footpath through the corn, where it was rather dusty.

At the church door stood an old crippled soldier leaning on a crutch. He had a wonderfully long beard, more red than white, and he bowed down to the ground and asked the old lady whether he might wipe her shoes. Then Karen put out her little foot too. "Dear me, what pretty dancing shoes!" said the soldier. "Sit fast, when you dance," said he, addressing the shoes, and slapping the soles with his hand. The old lady gave the soldier some money and then went with Karen into the church.

And all the people inside looked at Karen's red shoes, and all the figures gazed at them; when Karen knelt before the altar and put the golden goblet to her mouth, she thought only of the red shoes. It seemed to her as though they were swimming about in the goblet, and she forgot to sing the hymns, and forgot to say the Lord's Prayer.

Now everyone came out of church, and the old lady stepped into her carriage. But just as Karen was lifting up her foot to get in too, the old soldier said, "Dear me, what pretty dancing shoes!" and Karen could not help it, she was obliged to dance a few steps; and when she had once begun, her legs continued to dance. It seemed as if the shoes had got power over them. She danced around the church corner, for she could not stop; the coachman had to run after her and seize her. He lifted her into the carriage, but her feet continued to dance, so that she kicked the good old lady. They took off her shoes and her legs were at rest.

At home the shoes were put into the cupboard, but Karen could not help looking at them.

Now the old lady fell ill, and it was said that she would not rise from her bed again. She had to be nursed and waited upon, and this was no one's duty more than Karen's. But there was a grand ball in the town, and Karen was invited. She looked at the red shoes, saying to herself that there was no sin in doing that; she put the red shoes on, thinking there was no harm in that either; and then she went to the ball; and commenced to dance.

But when she wanted to go to the right, the shoes danced to the left, and when she wanted to dance up the room, the shoes danced down the room, down the stairs, through the street, and out through the gates of the town. She danced, and was obliged to dance, far out into the dark wood. Suddenly something shone up among the trees, and she believed it was the moon, for it was a face. But it was the old soldier with the red beard. He sat there nodding his head and said, "Dear me, what pretty dancing shoes!"

She was frightened, and wanted to throw the red shoes away, but they stuck fast. She tore off her

stockings, but the shoes had grown fast to her feet. She danced and was obliged to go on dancing over field and meadow, in rain and sunshine, by night and by day—but by night it was most horrible.

She danced out into the open churchyard; but the dead there did not dance. They had something better to do than that. She wanted to sit down on the pauper's grave where the bitter fern grows; but for her there was neither peace nor rest. And as she danced past the open church door she saw an angel there in long white robes, with wings reaching from his shoulders down to the earth. His face was stern and grave, and in his hand he held a broad, shining sword.

"Dance you shall," said he. "Dance in your red shoes till you are pale and cold, till your skin shrivels up and you are a skeleton! Dance you shall, from door to door, and where proud and wicked children live you shall knock, so that they may hear you and fear you! Dance you shall, dance!"

"Mercy!" cried Karen. But she did not hear what the angel answered, for the shoes carried her through the gate into the fields, along highways and byways, and unceasingly she had to dance.

One morning she danced past a door that she knew well. They were singing a hymn inside, and a coffin was being carried out covered with flowers. Then she knew that she was forsaken by everyone and damned by the angel of God.

She danced, and was obliged to go on dancing through the dark night. The shoes bore her away over thorns and stumps till she was all torn and bleeding; she danced away over the heath to a lonely little house. Here, she knew, lived the executioner, and she tapped at the window and said, "Come out, come out! I cannot come in, for I must dance."

And the executioner said, "I don't suppose you know who I am. I strike off the heads of the wicked, and I notice that my ax is tingling to do so."

"Don't cut off my head," said Karen, "for then I could not repent of my sin. But cut off my feet with the red shoes!"

And then she confessed her sin, and the executioner struck off her feet with the red shoes; but the shoes danced away with the little feet across the field into the deep forest.

Then he carved her a pair of wooden feet and

some crutches, and taught her a hymn that is always sung by sinners. She kissed the hand that guided the ax and went away.

"Now, I have suffered enough for the red shoes," she said; "I will go to church, so that people can see me." And she went quickly up to the church door; but when she got there, the red shoes were dancing before her, and she was frightened, and turned back.

During the whole week she was sad and wept many bitter tears, but when Sunday came again she said, "Now I have suffered and striven enough. I believe I am quite as good as many of those who sit in church and give themselves airs." And so she went boldly on;

but she had not got farther than the churchyard gate when she saw the red shoes dancing along before her. Then she became terrified, and turned back and repented right heartily of her sin.

She went to the parsonage, and begged that she might be taken into service there. She would be industrious, she said, and do everything that she could; she did not mind about the wages as long as she had a roof over her and was with good people. The pastor's wife had pity on her, and took her into service. And she was industrious and thoughtful. She sat quiet and listened when the pastor read aloud from the Bible in the evening. All the children liked her very much, but when they spoke about dress and grandeur and beauty she would shake her head.

On the following Sunday they all went to church, and she was asked whether she wished to go too; but, with tears in her eyes, she looked sadly at her crutches. And then the others went to hear God's Word, but she went alone into her little room; this was only large enough to hold the bed and a chair.

Here she sat down with her hymn book, and as she was reading it with a pious mind, the wind carried the notes of the organ over to her from the church, and in tears she lifted up her face and said, "O God, help me!"

Then the sun shone so brightly, and right before her stood an angel of God in white robes, it was the same one whom she had seen that night at the church door. He no longer carried the sharp sword, but a beautiful green branch, full of roses. With this he touched the ceiling, which rose up very high, and where he had touched it there shone a golden star. He touched the walls, which opened wide apart, and she saw the organ that was pealing forth; she saw the pictures of the old pastors and their wives, and the congregation sitting in the polished chairs and singing from their hymn books. The church itself had come to the poor girl in her narrow room, or the room had gone to the church. She sat in the pew with the rest of the pastor's household, and when they had finished the hymn and looked up, they nodded and said, "It was right of you to come, Karen."

"It was mercy," said she.

The organ played and the children's voices in the choir sounded soft and lovely. The bright, warm sunshine streamed through the window into the pew where Karen sat, and her heart became so filled with it, so filled with peace and joy, that it broke. Her soul flew on the sunbeams to heaven, and no one was there who asked after the red shoes.

The Snow Queen

An extract from the tale by Hans Christian Andersen

ONCE UPON A TIME there was a wicked sprite, who made a mirror that made all that was good and beautiful look poor and mean; while that which was good-for-nothing and ugly looked even more good-for-nothing and ugly. If a good thought passed through a man's mind, then a grin was seen in the mirror, and the sprite laughed heartily at his clever discovery. All the little sprites thought they would fly up to the sky and have a joke there. The higher they flew with the mirror, the more terribly it grinned: they could hardly hold it fast—suddenly it shook so

terribly with grinning, that it flew out of their hands
and fell to the earth, where it was dashed in a
hundred million and more pieces. And now it worked
much more evil than before; for some of these pieces
were hardly so large as a grain of sand, and they flew
into people's eyes and then people were attracted to
that which was evil. Some persons even got a splinter
in their heart, and then their heart became like a
lump of ice. Many of the splinters were carried aloft
by the air, and then blown about the wide world...

    At this time, there lived in a large town two little

children—a boy called Kay and a girl named Gerda. They were not brother and sister; but they cared for each other as much as if they were. Their houses were next to each other—and there was to the roof of each house a small window. In summer, when the windows were open they could get to each other with one jump over the gutter. The children liked nothing more than to sit together at the windows and talk, holding each other by the hand, often kissing the roses in their window boxes and looking up at the clear sunshine.

One day, Kay and Gerda were at the windows, looking at a picture book, when Kay said, "Oh! I feel such a sharp pain in my heart; and now something has got into my eye!"

The little girl put her arms around his neck. He winked his eyes; now there was nothing to be seen.

"I think it is out now," said he, but it was not. It was just one of those pieces of glass from the magic mirror that had got into his eye; and poor Kay had got another piece right in his heart.

"You look so ugly!" he suddenly said to Gerda. "And these roses are very ugly, just like the boxes they are planted in!" And then he gave a box a good kick with his foot, and pulled a rose up.

"What are you doing?" cried the little girl; and as he perceived her fright, he pulled up another rose, got in at the window, and hastened off.

Afterward, he was able to imitate the gait and manner of everyone in the street. Everything that was peculiar and displeasing in them, Kay knew how to imitate, and make everybody laugh—except the person being made fun of! But it was the glass he had got in his eye; the glass that was sticking in his heart, which made him tease even little Gerda, whose whole soul was devoted to him.

One winter's day, when flakes of snow were flying about, he spread the skirts of his blue coat, and caught the snow as it fell.

"Look through this glass, Gerda," said he. And every flake seemed larger, and appeared like a magnificent flower, or a beautiful star; it was splendid to look at!

"Look, how clever!" said Kay. "That's much more interesting than real flowers!"

It was not long after this, that Kay came one day with large gloves on, and his little sledge at his back, and bawled into Gerda's ears, "I have permission to go out into the square where the others are playing." And off he was in a moment.

There, in the market place, some of the boldest boys used to tie their sleds to the carts as they passed by, and so they were pulled along, and got a good ride. Soon a large sled passed by: it was painted quite white, and there was someone in it wrapped up in a rough white mantle of fur, with a rough white fur cap on his head. The sled drove round the square twice, and Kay tied on his sled as quickly as he could, and off he drove with it. On they went quicker and quicker into the next street; and the person who drove turned around to Kay and nodded to him in a friendly manner, just as if they knew each other. Every time he was going to untie his sled, the person nodded to him, and then Kay sat quiet; and so on they went till they came outside the gates of the town. Then the snow began to fall so thickly that the little boy could not see an arm's length before him, but still on he went. Suddenly he let go of the string he held in his hand in order to get loose from the sled, but it was no use; still the little vehicle rushed on with the quickness of the wind. He then cried as loud as he could, but no one heard him; the snow drifted and the sled flew on, and sometimes it gave a jerk as though they were driving over hedges and ditches. Kay was quite frightened, and he tried to

repeat the Lord's Prayer; but he was only able to remember his times tables.

The snowflakes grew larger and larger, till at last they looked just like great white fowls. Suddenly they flew on one side; the large sled stopped, and the person who drove rose up. It was a lady; her cloak and cap were of snow. She was tall and of slender figure, and of a dazzling whiteness. It was the Snow Queen.

"We have traveled fast," said she; "but it is freezing cold. Come under my bearskin." And she put him in the sled beside her, wrapped the fur around him, and he felt as though he were sinking in a snow drift.

"Are you still cold?" asked she, and then she kissed his forehead. Ah! It was colder than ice; it penetrated to his very heart, which was already almost a frozen lump. It seemed to him as if he were about to die—but a moment more and it was quite congenial to him, and he did not notice the cold that was around him.

"My sled! Do not forget my sled!" It was the first thing he thought of. It was there tied to one of the white chickens, who flew along with it on his back behind the large sled. The Snow Queen kissed Kay once more, and then he forgot little Gerda, grandmother, and all whom he had left at his home.

Kay thought she was very beautiful. In his eyes she was perfect, and he did not fear her at all. He looked upward in the large, huge empty space above him, and on she flew with him; flew high over the black clouds, while the storm moaned and whistled as though it were singing some old tune. On they flew over woods and lakes, over seas, and many lands, and beneath them the chilling storm rushed fast, the wolves howled, the snow crackled. Above them flew large screaming crows, but higher up appeared the moon, quite large and bright, and it was on it that Kay gazed during the long, long winter's night, while by day he slept at the feet of the Snow Queen.

What became of little Gerda when Kay did not return? Where could he be? Nobody knew, nobody could give any information. All the boys knew was that they had seen him tie his sled to another large, splendid one, which drove down the street and out of the town. Nobody knew where he was. Many sad tears were shed, and Gerda wept long and bitterly.

At last she said that he must have been drowned in the river that flowed close to the town—that alas, he must be dead!

The Rose Tree

From *English Fairy Tales* by Joseph Jacobs

THERE WAS ONCE a good man who had two children: a girl by a first wife, and a boy by the second. The girl was as white as milk and her lips were like cherries. Her hair was like golden silk and it hung to the ground. Her brother loved her dearly, but her wicked stepmother hated her.

"Child," said the stepmother one day, "go to the grocer's and buy me a pound of candles." She gave her the money, and the little girl went, bought the candles, and started on her return. There was a stile to cross. She put down the candles whilst she got over. Up came a dog and ran off with the candles.

She went back to the grocer's and she got a second bunch. She came to the stile, set down the candles, and proceeded to climb over. Up came the dog and ran off with the candles.

She went again to the grocer's and she got a third bunch, and just the same happened. Then she came to her stepmother crying, for she had spent all the money and had lost three bunches of candles.

The stepmother was angry, but she pretended not to mind the loss. She said to the child, "Come, lay your head on my lap that I may comb your hair." So the little one laid her head in the woman's lap, who proceeded to comb the yellow silken hair. And when she combed the hair fell over her knees and rolled right down to the ground.

Then the stepmother hated her more for the beauty of her hair, so she said to her, "I cannot part your hair on my knee, fetch me a block of wood." So the little girl fetched it. Then said the stepmother, "I cannot part your hair with a comb, fetch me an ax."

So the little girl fetched it.

"Now," said the wicked woman, "lay your head down on the block whilst I part your hair."

Well! She laid down her little golden head without fear; and whist! Down came the ax, and it was off. So the stepmother wiped the ax and laughed.

Then she took the heart and liver of the little girl, and she stewed them and brought them into the house for supper. The husband tasted them and

shook his head. He said they tasted very strange. She gave some to the little boy, but he would not eat. She tried to force him, but he refused, and ran out into the garden, and took up his little sister, and put her in a box, and buried the box under a rose tree. Every day he went to the tree and wept, till his tears ran down on the box.

One day the rose tree flowered. It was spring, and there among the flowers was a bird, and it sang, and sang, and sang like an angel out of heaven. Away it flew, and it went to a cobbler's shop, and perched itself on a tree close by and thus it sang,

> "*My wicked mother slew me,*
> *My dear father ate me,*
> *My little brother whom I love*
> *Sits below, and I sing above*
> *Stick, stock, stone dead.*"

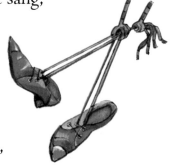

"Sing again that beautiful song," asked the shoemaker.

"If you will first give me those little red shoes you are making," said the bird. The cobbler gave the shoes,

and the bird sang the song then flew to a tree in front
of a watchmaker's, and sang:

   "My wicked mother slew me,
     My dear father ate me,
     My little brother whom I love
     Sits below, and I sing above
      Stick, stock, stone dead."

"Oh, the beautiful song! Sing it again, sweet bird,"
asked the watchmaker.

"If you will give me first that gold watch and chain
in your hand," said the bird. The jeweler gave the
watch and chain. The bird took it in one foot, the
shoes in the other, and, after having repeated the
song, flew away to where three millers were picking a
millstone. The bird perched on a tree and sang:

   "My wicked mother slew me,
     My dear father ate me,
     My little brother whom I love
     Sits below, and I sing above
      Stick!"

Then one of the men put down his tool and

looked up from his work, "*Stock!*"

Then the second miller's man laid aside his tool and looked up, "*Stone!*"

Then the third miller's man laid down his tool and looked up, "*Dead!*"

Then all three cried out with one voice: "Oh, what a beautiful song! Sing it, sweet bird, again."

"If you will put the millstone around my neck," said the bird. The men did what the bird wanted and away to the tree it flew with the millstone around its neck, the red shoes in one foot, and the gold watch and chain in the other. It sang the song and then flew home. It rattled the millstone against the eaves of the house, and the stepmother said, "It thunders." Then the little boy ran out to see the thunder, and down dropped the red shoes at his feet. The bird rattled the millstone against the eaves of the house once more, and the stepmother said again, "It thunders." Then the father ran out and down fell the watch and chain about his neck.

In ran the father and son, laughing and saying,

"See, what fine things the thunder has brought us!"
Then the bird rattled the millstone against the eaves of the house a third time; and the stepmother said, "It thunders, perhaps the thunder has brought something for me," and she ran out. But the moment she stepped outside the door, down fell the millstone on her head, and so she died.

Bluebeard

After Charles Perrault,
from Andrew Lang's *Blue Fairy Book*

T HERE WAS A MAN who had fine houses, both in
town and country, a great deal of silver and gold
treasures, fancy furniture, and many grand coaches.
But this man was so unlucky as to have a blue beard,
which made him so frightfully ugly that all the
women and girls turned away from him.

One of his neighbors, a noble lady, had two
daughters who were perfect beauties. He desired one
of them in marriage, leaving to her the choice of
which of the two she would give to him. However,
they would neither of them have him, and sent him

backward and forward from one another, not being able to bear the thought of marrying a man who had a blue beard. Besides this, what made them most put off was that he had already been married to several wives who had disappeared, and nobody ever found out what became of them.

To win them over, Bluebeard took them, with their mother and a few of their friends, along with other young people of the neighborhood, to one of his country mansions—here they stayed a whole week.

The entire time was spent in pleasurable pursuits: hunting, fishing, dancing, mirth, and feasting. Nobody went to bed, but all passed the night in chatting and joking with each other. In short, everything succeeded so well that the youngest daughter began to think the master of the house not to have a beard so very blue, and that he was a most agreeable gentleman.

As soon as they returned home, the marriage took place amid great celebrations and feasting. The newlyweds settled into enjoying life together until, about a month after the wedding, Bluebeard told his wife that he had to go on a business trip for at least six weeks. He wanted her to have fun while he was away, to send for her friends and to take them to the country mansion, if she pleased, but to make good cheer wherever she was.

"Here," said he, "are the keys of the two great stores wherein I have my best furniture; these are of my silver and gold treasures; these open my strong boxes, which hold my money; these my caskets of jewels; and this is the master-key to all my rooms. But for this little one here, it is the key of the cupboard at the end of the great hall on the ground floor. Open them all; go into all and every one of them, except that little cupboard, which I forbid you—and I mean that so seriously that, if you happen to open it, you will feel the full force of my anger."

She promised to observe, very exactly, what he had ordered. Then he, after having embraced her, got into his coach and proceeded on his journey.

Her neighbors and good friends did not wait to be

sent for by the new married lady, so great was their
impatience to see all the rich furniture of her house,
not daring to come while her husband was there,
because of his blue beard, which frightened them.
They ran through all the rooms, cupboards,
and stores, which were all so fine and rich that they
seemed to surpass one another.

After that they went up into the two great stores
where the best and richest furniture was; they couldn't
admire enough the number and beauty of the
tapestries, beds, couches, cabinets, stands, tables, and
mirrors, in which you might see yourself from head
to foot; the finest and most magnificent that ever
were to be seen.

In the meantime, their newly married friend did
not enjoy any of these rich things, because of the
impatience she had to go and open the cupboard on
the ground floor. She was so much pressed by her
curiosity that, without considering that it was very
impolite to leave her company, she went down a little
back staircase, and with such haste that she stumbled

two or three times and could have
fallen and broken her neck.

Coming to the cupboard door,
she hesitated for some time,
thinking upon her husband's
orders, and considering what fury
might befall her if she was
disobedient; but the temptation
was so strong she could not
overcome it. She then took the
little key and opened the
cupboard door, trembling.

At first she could not see
anything clearly because the
windows were shut. After
some moments she began to make out that the floor
was all covered over with blood, on which lay the
bodies of several dead women, ranged against the
walls. These were all the wives whom Bluebeard had
married and murdered, one after another.

She thought she should have died for fear, and the

key, which she had pulled out of the lock, fell out of her hand.

After having somewhat recovered her surprise, she took up the key, locked the door, and went upstairs into her chamber to recover herself, but she could not, she was so much frightened. Having observed that the key of the cupboard was stained with blood, she tried two or three times to wipe it off, but the blood would not come out; in vain did she wash it, and even rub it with soap and sand—the blood still remained, for the key was magical, and she could never make it quite clean; when the blood was gone off from one side, it came again on the other.

When Bluebeard returned from his journey, his wife did all she could to convince him she was extremely glad of his return.

Next morning he asked her for the keys, which she gave him, but with such a trembling hand that he easily guessed what had happened.

"What!" said he. "Isn't the key of my cupboard among the rest?"

"I must certainly have left it above, upon the table," said she.

"Fail not to bring it to me presently," said he.

After several goings backward and forward she was forced to bring him the key. Bluebeard, having very attentively considered it, said to his wife, "How come there is blood upon the key?"

"I do not know," cried the poor woman. She was paler than death.

"You do not know!" replied Bluebeard. "I very well know. You were determined to go into the cupboard, were you not? Mighty well, madam; you shall go in, and take your place among the ladies you saw there."

Upon this she threw herself at her husband's feet, and begged his pardon with all the signs of true repentance, vowing that she would never more be disobedient. She would have melted a rock, so beautiful and sorrowful was she; but Bluebeard had a heart harder than any rock!

"You must die straightaway, madam," said he.

"Since I must die," answered she, looking upon him with her eyes all bathed in tears, "give me some little time to say my prayers."

"I give you," replied Bluebeard, "a quarter of an hour, but not one moment more."

When she was alone she called out to her sister, and said to her: "Anne," for that was her name, "go up, I beg you, upon the top of the tower, and look if my brothers are not coming over; they promised me that they would come today, and if you see them, give them a sign to make haste."

Her sister Anne went up upon the top of the tower, and the poor wife cried out from time to time, "Anne, do you see anyone coming?"

And Anne said, "I see nothing but the sun, which makes a dust, and the grass, which looks green."

In the meanwhile, Bluebeard, holding a great sword in his hand, cried out as loud as he could bawl, "Come down instantly, or I shall come up to you."

"One moment longer, if you please," said his wife, and then she cried out very softly, "Anne, do you see anybody coming?"

And Anne answered, "I see nothing but the sun, which makes a dust, and the grass, which is green."

"Come down quickly," cried Bluebeard, "or I will come up to you."

"I am coming," answered his wife, and then she cried, "Anne, do you not see anyone coming?"

"I see," replied Anne, "a great dust, which comes on this side here."

"Are they my brothers?"

"Alas! No, my dear sister, I see a flock of sheep."

"Come down!" roared Bluebeard.

"One moment longer," said his wife, and then she cried out, "Anne, do you see nobody coming?"

"I see," said she, "two horsemen, but they are yet a great way off."

"God be praised," replied the poor wife joyfully, "they are my brothers; I will make them a sign, as well as I can, for them to make haste."

Then Bluebeard bawled out so loud that he made the whole house tremble. The distressed wife came down, and threw herself at his feet, all in tears, with her hair about her shoulders.

"This makes no difference," says Bluebeard; "you must die." Then, taking hold of her hair with one hand, and lifting up the sword with the other, he was going to take off her head. The poor lady, turning about to him, and looking at him with dying eyes,

asked him to give her one little moment to recollect herself. "No, no," said he, "recommend yourself to God," and he was just ready to strike when at that very instant there was such a loud knocking at the gate that Bluebeard made a sudden stop.

The gate was opened, and presently entered two horsemen, who, drawing their swords, ran directly to Bluebeard. He knew them to be his wife's brothers, one a dragoon, the other a musketeer, so he ran away immediately to save himself; but the two brothers pursued so close that they overtook him before he could get to the steps of the porch. The brothers ran their swords through Bluebeard's body and left him dead. The poor wife was almost as dead as her husband, and had not strength enough to rise and welcome her brothers.

Bluebeard had no heirs, and so his wife became mistress of all his estate. She made use of one part of it to marry her sister Anne to a young gentleman who had loved her a long while, another part to buy captains' commissions for her brothers, and the rest to marry herself to a very worthy gentleman, who made her forget all about the ill time she had passed with Bluebeard.

The Devil and his Grandmother

By the Brothers Grimm

T HERE WAS A GREAT WAR, and the king had many soldiers, but gave them small pay, so small that they could not live upon it, so three of them agreed among themselves to desert. One of them said to the others, "If we are caught we shall be hanged on the gallows, how shall we avoid it?"

Another said, "Look at that great cornfield, if we were to hide ourselves there, no one could find us; the troops are not allowed to enter it, and tomorrow they are to march away."

They crept into the corn, only the troops did not

march away, but remained lying all round about it. They stayed in the corn for two days and two nights, and were so hungry that they all but died, but if they had come out, their death would have been certain. Then said they, "What is the use of our deserting if we have to perish miserably here?"

But now a fiery dragon came flying through the air, and it came down to them, and asked why they had hidden themselves there. They answered, "We are three soldiers who have deserted because the pay was so bad, and now we shall have to die of hunger if we stay here, or to dangle on the gallows if we go out."

"If you will serve me for seven years," said the dragon, "I will carry you through the army so that no one shall seize you."

"We have no choice, so we have to accept," the soldiers replied.

Then the dragon caught hold of them with its claws, and carried them away through the air over the army, and put them down again on the earth far from it; but the dragon was no other than the Devil. He gave them a small whip and said, "Whip with it and crack it, and then as much gold will spring up around about as you can wish for; then you can live like great lords, keep horses, and drive your carriages, but when the seven years have come to an end, you are my property." Then he put in front of them a book that they were all three forced to sign. "I will, however, then set you a riddle," said the dragon, "and if you can guess that, you shall be free, and released from my power."

Then the dragon flew away from them, and they went away with their whip, had gold in plenty, ordered themselves rich clothes, and traveled about the world. Wherever they were they lived in pleasure and magnificence, rode on horseback, drove in carriages, ate and drank, but did nothing wicked.

The time slipped quickly away, and when the seven years were coming to an end, two of them were terribly anxious and alarmed; but the third took matters easily, and said, "Brothers, fear nothing, my head is sharp enough, I shall guess the riddle." They went out into the open country and sat down, and the two pulled sorrowful faces.

Then an aged woman came up to them who enquired why they were so sad.

"Alas!" said they. "How can that concern you? After all, you cannot help us."

"Who knows?" she replied. "Confide your trouble to me."

So they told her that they had been the Devil's servants for nearly seven years, and that he had provided them with gold as plentifully as if it had been blackberries, but that they had sold themselves to him, and were forfeited to him, if at the end of the seven years they could not guess a riddle.

The old woman said, "If you are to be saved, one of you must go into the forest, there he will come to a fallen rock that looks like a little house, he must enter that, and then he will obtain help."

The two melancholy ones thought to themselves, 'That will still not save us,' and stayed where they were, but the third, the merry one, got up and walked on in the forest until he found the rock house.

In the little house, however, a very aged woman was sitting, who was the Devil's grandmother, and asked the soldier where he came from, and what he wanted there. He told her everything that had happened and, as he pleased her well, she had pity on him, and said she would help him. She lifted up a great stone that lay above a cellar, and said, "Hide yourself there, you can hear everything that is said here; only sit still, and do not stir. When the dragon comes, I will question him about the riddle. He tells everything to me, so listen carefully to his answer."

At twelve o'clock at night, the dragon came flying there and asked for his dinner. The grandmother laid the table and served up food and drink, so that he was pleased, and they ate and drank together. In the course of conversation, she asked him what kind of a day he had had, and how many souls he had got?

"Nothing went very well today," he answered, "but I have laid hold of three soldiers, I have them safe."

"Indeed! Three soldiers, that's something like, but they may escape you yet."

The Devil said mockingly, "They are mine! I will set them a riddle, which they will never in this world be able to guess!"

"What riddle is that?" she enquired.

"I will tell you. In the great North Sea lies a dead dogfish, that shall be your roast meat, and the rib of a whale shall be your silver spoon, and a hollow old horse's hoof shall be your wine glass."

When the Devil had gone to bed, the old grandmother raised up the stone and let out the soldier. "Did you pay careful attention to everything?" she asked.

"Yes," said he, "I know enough."

Then he had to go back another way, through the window, secretly and with all speed to his companions. He told them how the Devil had been tricked by the old grandmother, and how he had learned the answer to the riddle from him. Then they were all joyous and of good cheer, and took the whip and whipped so much gold for themselves that it ran all over the ground.

When the seven years had fully gone by, the Devil came with the book, showed the signatures, and said, "I will take you with me to hell. There you shall have a meal. If you can guess what kind of roast meat you will have to eat, you shall be free and released from your bargain, and may keep the whip as well."

Then the first soldier began and said, "In the great North Sea lies a dead dogfish, that no doubt is the roast meat."

The Devil was angry, and began to mutter, "Hm! Hm! Hm!" And he asked the second, "But what will your spoon be?"

"The rib of a whale, that is to be our silver spoon."

The Devil made a wry face, again growled, "Hm! Hm! Hm!" and said to the third, "And do you also know what your wine glass is to be?"

"An old horse's hoof is to be our wine glass."

Then the Devil flew away with a loud cry, and had no more power over them, but the three kept the whip, whipped as much money for themselves with it as they wanted, and lived happily to their end.

The Ratcatcher

From Andrew Lang's *Red Fairy Book*

A VERY LONG TIME AGO the town of Hamel in Germany was invaded by bands of rats, the like of which had never been seen before nor will ever be seen again.

They were great black creatures that ran boldly in broad daylight through the streets, and swarmed all over the houses, so that people could not put their hand or foot down anywhere without touching one. When dressing in the morning they found them in their breeches and petticoats, in their pockets and in their boots; and when they wanted a morsel to eat, the voracious horde had swept away everything from cellar to garret. The night was even worse. As soon as the lights were out, these untiring nibblers set to work. And everywhere, in the ceilings, in the floors, in the cupboards, at the doors, there was a chase and a rummage, and so furious a noise, that a deaf man could not have rested for one hour together.

Doom and Death

Neither cats nor dogs, nor poison nor traps, nor prayers nor candles burned to all the saints—nothing would do anything. The more they killed the more came. And the inhabitants of Hamel began to go to the dogs (not that *they* were of much use), when one Friday there arrived in the town a man with a queer face, who played the bagpipes and sang this refrain:

"*Qui vivra verra:*

Le voila,

Le preneur des rats."

He was a great gawky fellow, dry and bronzed, with a crooked nose, a long rat-tail moustache, two great yellow piercing and mocking eyes, under a large felt hat set off by a scarlet feather. He was dressed in a green jacket with a leather belt and red breeches, and on his feet were sandals fastened by thongs passed round his legs in the gipsy fashion. That is how he may be seen to this day, painted on a window of the cathedral of Hamel.

He stopped on the great market place before the town hall, turned his back on the church and went on with his music, singing:

"Who lives shall see:
    This is he,
    The ratcatcher."

The town council had just assembled to consider once more this plague, from which no one could save the town.

The stranger sent word to the counselors that, if they would make it worth his while, he would rid them of all their rats before night, down to the very last one.

"Then he is a sorcerer!" cried the citizens with one voice. "We must beware of him."

The Town Counselor, who was considered clever, reassured them.

He said: "Sorcerer or not, if this piper speaks the truth, it was he who sent us this horrible vermin that he wants to rid us of today for money. Well, we must learn to catch the Devil in his own snares. You leave it to me."

"Leave it to the Town Counselor," said the citizens

one to another.

And the stranger was brought before them.

"Before night," said the stranger, "I shall have despatched all the rats in Hamel if you will but pay me a gros a head."

"A gros a head!" cried the citizens. "But that will come to millions of florins!"

The Town Counselor simply shrugged his shoulders and said to the stranger, "A bargain! To work; the rats will be paid one gros a head."

The bagpiper announced that he would operate that very evening when the moon rose. He added that the inhabitants should at that hour leave the streets free, and content themselves with looking out of their windows at what was passing, and that it would be a pleasant spectacle.

When the people of Hamel heard of the bargain, they too exclaimed, "A gros a head! But this will cost us a great deal of money!"

"Leave it to the Town Counselor," said the town council with a malicious air. And the good people of

Hamel repeated with their counselors, "Leave it to the Town Counselor."

Toward nine at night the bagpiper reappeared on the market place. He turned, as at first, his back on the church, and the moment the moon rose on the horizon, "Trarira, trari!" the bagpipes resounded.

It was first a slow, caressing sound, then more and more lively and urgent, and so sonorous and piercing that it penetrated as far as the farthest alleys and retreats of the town.

Soon from the bottom of the cellars, the top of the garrets, from under all the furniture, from all the nooks and corners of the houses, out come the rats, search for the door, fling themselves into the street, and trip, trip, trip, begin to run in file toward the front of the town hall, so squeezed together that they covered the pavement like waves.

When the square was quite full the bagpiper faced about, and, still playing briskly, turned toward the river that runs at the foot of the walls of Hamel.

When he arrived there he turned around; the rats

were following.

"Hop! Hop!" he cried, pointing with his finger to the middle of the stream, where the water whirled and was drawn down as if through a funnel. And hop! Hop! Without hesitating, the rats took the leap, swam straight to the funnel, plunged in head foremost and disappeared.

The plunging continued till midnight.

At last, dragging himself with difficulty, came a big

rat, white with age, and it stopped on the bank. It was the king of the band.

"Are they all there, friend Blanchet?" the bagpiper asked the big rat.

"They are all there," replied friend Blanchet.

"And how many were they?"

"Nine hundred and ninety thousand, nine hundred and ninety-nine."

"Then go and join them, old sire, and au revoir."

Then the old white rat sprang in his turn into the river, swam to the whirlpool and disappeared.

When the bagpiper had thus concluded his business he went to bed at his inn. And for the first time during three months the people of Hamel slept quietly through the night.

The next morning, at nine o'clock, the bagpiper went to the town hall, where the town council were waiting for him.

"All your rats took a jump into the river yesterday," said he to the counsellors, "and I guarantee that not one of them comes back. They were nine hundred and ninety thousand, nine hundred and ninety-nine, at one gros a head. Reckon!"

"Let us reckon the heads first. One gros a head is one head the gros. Where are the heads?"

The ratcatcher did not expect this treacherous stroke. He paled with anger and his eyes flashed fire. "The heads!" cried he. "If you care about them, go and find them in the river."

"So," replied the Town Counselor, "you refuse to hold to the terms of your agreement? We ourselves could refuse you all payment. But you have been of use to us, and we will not let you go without a recompense," and he offered him fifty crowns.

"Keep your recompense for yourself," replied the ratcatcher proudly. "If you do not pay me I will be paid by your heirs."

Thereupon he pulled his hat down over his eyes, went hastily out of the hall, and left the town without speaking to a soul.

When the Hamel people heard how the affair had ended they rubbed their hands, and with no more scruple than their Town Counselor, they laughed over the ratcatcher, who, they said, was caught in his own trap. But what made them laugh above all was his threat of getting himself paid by their heirs. Ha! They wished that they only had such creditors for the rest of their lives.

Next day, which was a Sunday, they all went gaily to church, thinking that after Mass they would at last be able to eat some good thing that the rats had not tasted before them. They never suspected the terrible surprise that awaited them on their return home. No children anywhere—they had all disappeared!

"Our children! Where are our poor children?" was the cry that was soon heard in all the streets.

Then through the east door of the town came three children, who cried and wept, and this is what they told. While the parents were at church a wonderful music had resounded. Soon all the little boys and all the little girls that had been left at home had gone out, attracted by the magic sounds, and had rushed to the great market place. There they found the ratcatcher playing his bagpipes at the same spot as the evening before. Then the stranger had begun to walk quickly, and they had followed, running, singing, and dancing to the sound of the music, as far as the foot of the mountain which one sees on entering Hamel. At their approach the mountain had opened a little, and the bagpiper and children had gone in, after which it had closed again. Only the three little ones who told the adventure had remained outside, as if by a miracle. One was bandy-legged and could not run fast enough; the other, who had left the house in haste, one foot shod the other bare, had hurt himself against a big stone and could not walk without difficulty; the third had arrived in time, but in hurrying to go in with the others, had struck so violently against the wall of the mountain that he fell backward at the moment it closed.

At this story the parents redoubled their lamentations. They ran with pikes and mattocks to the mountain, and searched till evening to find the opening by which their children had disappeared,

without being able to find it. At last, the night falling, they returned desolate to Hamel.

But the most unhappy of all was the Town Counselor, for he lost three little boys and two pretty little girls, and to crown all, the people of Hamel overwhelmed him with reproaches, forgetting that the evening before they had all agreed with him.

What had become of all these children?

The parents always hoped they were not dead, and that the ratcatcher, who certainly must have come out of the mountain, would have taken them with him to his country. That is why for several years they went in search of them to different countries, but no one ever came on the trace of the poor little ones.

The King who would see Paradise

From Andrew Lang's *Orange Fairy Book*

ONCE UPON A TIME there was a king who, one day out hunting, came upon a holy man, or fakeer, in a lonely place in the mountains. The fakeer was seated on a little old bedstead reading the Koran, with his patched cloak thrown over his shoulders.

The king asked him what he was reading; and he said he was reading about Paradise, and praying that he might be worthy to enter there. Then they began to talk, and the king asked the fakeer if he could show him a glimpse of Paradise, for he found it impossible to believe in what he could not see. The fakeer replied that he was asking a very difficult, and perhaps a very dangerous, thing; but that he would pray for him, and perhaps he might be able to do it; only he warned the king both against the dangers of his unbelief, and against the curiosity that prompted him to ask this thing. However, the king was not to be swayed, and he promised the fakeer always to provide him with food, if he, in return, would pray for him. To this the fakeer agreed, and so they parted.

Time went on, and the king always sent the old fakeer his food according to his promise; but, whenever he sent to ask him when he was going to show him Paradise, the fakeer always replied, "Not yet, not yet!"

After a year or two had passed, the king heard one day that the fakeer was very ill—indeed, believed to be dying. Instantly he hurried off and found that it was really true, and that the fakeer was even then breathing his last. There and then the king besought him to remember his promise, and to show him a glimpse of Paradise. The dying fakeer replied that if the king would come to his funeral and, when the grave was filled in, and everyone else was gone away, he would come and lay his hand upon the grave, he would keep his word, and show him a glimpse of Paradise. At the same time he implored the king not to do this thing, but to be content to see Paradise when God called him there. Still the king's curiosity was so aroused that he would not give way.

Accordingly, after the fakeer was dead and had been buried, the king stayed behind when all the rest went away; and then, when he was quite alone, he stepped forward, and laid his hand upon the grave! Instantly the ground opened and the astonished king, peeping in, saw a flight of rough steps, and, at the bottom of them, the fakeer sitting, just as he used to sit, on his rickety bedstead, reading the Koran!

At first the king was so surprised and frightened that he could only stare; but the fakeer beckoned to him to come down, so, mustering up his courage, he boldly stepped down into the grave.

The fakeer rose and, making a sign to the king to

DOOM AND DEATH

follow, walked a few paces along a dark passage. Then he stopped, turned solemnly to his companion, and, with a movement of his hand, drew aside as it were a heavy curtain, and revealed—what? No one knows what was there shown to the king, nor did he ever tell anyone; but, when the fakeer at length dropped the curtain, and the king turned to leave the place, he had had his glimpse of Paradise! Trembling in every limb, he staggered back along the passage, and stumbled up the steps out of the tomb into the fresh air again.

The dawn was breaking. It seemed odd to the king that he had been so long in the grave. It appeared but a few minutes ago that he had descended, passed along a few steps to the place where he had peeped beyond the curtain, and returned again after perhaps five minutes of that wonderful view! And what was it he had seen? He racked his brains to remember, but he could not call to mind a single thing! How curious everything looked too! His own city, which by now he was entering, seemed changed and strange to him! The sun was already up when he turned into the palace gate and entered the hall. It was full; a chamberlain came across and asked him why he sat unbidden in the king's presence. "But I am the king!" he cried.

"What king?" said the chamberlain.

"The true king of this country," said he indignantly.

Then the chamberlain went away, and spoke to the king who sat on the throne, and the old king heard words like "mad," "age," "compassion." Then the king on the throne called him to come forward and, as he went, he caught sight of himself reflected in the polished steel shield of the bodyguard, and he started back in horror! He was old, decrepit, dirty, and ragged! His long white beard and locks were unkempt, and straggled all over his chest and shoulders. Only one sign of royalty remained to him, and that was the signet ring upon his right hand. He dragged it off with shaking fingers and held it up to the king.

"Tell me who I am," the old king cried, "there is my signet, who once sat where you sit—even yesterday!"

The king looked at him compassionately, and examined the signet with curiosity. Then he commanded, and they brought out dusty records and archives of the kingdom, and old coins of previous reigns, and compared them faithfully. At last the king turned to the old man and said, "Old man, such a king as this whose signet you have, reigned seven hundred years ago; but he is said to have disappeared, none know whither; where got you the ring?"

Then the old man cried and wailed, for he understood that he, who was not content to wait patiently to see the Paradise of the faithful, had been judged already. And he turned and left the hall without a word, and went into the jungle, where he lived for twenty-five years a life of prayer and meditation, until at last the Angel of Death came to him, and mercifully released him, purged and purified through his punishment.

The Singing Bone

By the Brothers Grimm

I N A CERTAIN COUNTRY there was once great lamentation over a wild boar that laid waste the farmer's fields, killed the cattle, and ripped up people's bodies with its tusks. The king promised a large reward to anyone who would free the land from this plague; but the beast was so big and strong that no one dared to go near the forest in which it lived. At last the king gave notice that whosoever should capture or kill the wild boar should have his only daughter for his wife.

Now there lived in the country two brothers, sons

of a poor man, who declared themselves willing to undertake the hazardous enterprise; the elder, who was crafty and shrewd, out of pride; the younger, who was innocent and simple, from a kind heart.

The king said, "In order that you may be the more sure of finding the beast, you must go into the forest from opposite sides."

So the elder went in on the west side, and the younger on the east.

When the younger had gone a short way, a little man stepped up to him. He held in his hand a spear and said, "I give you this spear because your heart is pure and good; with this you can boldly attack the wild boar, and it will do you no harm."

The younger brother thanked the little man, shouldered the spear, and went on fearlessly.

Before long he saw the beast, which rushed at him; but he held the spear toward it, and in its blind fury it ran so swiftly against it that its heart was split in two.

Then he took the monster on his back and went homeward with it to the king.

As he came out at the other side of the wood, there stood at the entrance a house where people were making merry with wine and dancing. His elder brother had gone in here, and, thinking that after all the boar would not run away from him, was going to drink until he felt brave. But when he saw his young brother coming out of the wood laden with his booty, his envious, evil heart gave him no peace. He called out to him, "Come in, dear brother, rest and refresh yourself with a cup of wine."

The youth, who suspected no evil, went in and told him about the good little man who had given him the spear wherewith he had slain the boar.

The elder brother kept him there until the evening,

and then they went away together, and when in the darkness they came to a bridge over a brook, the elder brother let the other go first. When the younger brother was halfway across, the elder brother gave him such a blow from behind that the younger fell down dead. The elder buried him beneath the bridge, took the boar, and carried it to the king, pretending that he had killed it; whereupon he obtained the king's daughter in marriage. And when his younger brother did not come back he said, "The boar must have killed him," and every one believed it.

But as nothing remains hidden from God, so this black deed also was to come to light.

Years afterward a shepherd was driving his herd across the bridge, and saw lying in the sand beneath, a snow-white little bone. He thought that it would make a good mouthpiece, so he clambered down, picked it up, and cut out of it a mouthpiece for his horn. But when he blew through it the first time, to his great astonishment, the bone began of its own accord to sing:

The Singing Bone

"Ah, friend, thou blowest upon my bone!
  Long have I lain beside the water;
  My brother slew me for the boar,
  And took for his wife the king's daughter."
"What a wonderful horn!" said the shepherd. "It
sings by itself, I must take it to my lord the king."
And when he came with it to the king the horn again
began to sing its little song. The king understood it
all, and caused the ground below the bridge to be dug
up, and then the whole skeleton of the murdered man
came to light. The wicked brother could not deny the
deed, and was sewn up in a sack and drowned. But
the bones of the murdered man were laid to rest in a
beautiful tomb in the churchyard.

Gold-tree and Silver-tree

A Snow White story from Joseph Jacobs' *Celtic Fairy Tales*

ONCE UPON A TIME there was a king who had a wife, whose name was Silver-tree, and a daughter, whose name was Gold-tree. On a certain day of the days, Gold-tree and Silver-tree went to a glen where there was a well, and in it there was a trout.

Said Silver-tree, "Troutie, pretty little fellow, am not I the most beautiful queen in the world?"

"Oh! Indeed you are not."

"Who then?"

"Why, Gold-tree, your daughter."

Silver-tree went home, blind with rage. She lay down on the bed, and vowed she would never be well until she could get the heart and the liver of Gold-tree, her daughter, to eat.

At nightfall the king came home, and it was told him that Silver-tree, his wife, was very ill. He went where she was, and asked her what was wrong.

"Oh! Only a thing that you may heal if you like."

"Oh! Indeed there is nothing at all which I could do for you that I would not do."

"If I get the heart and the liver of Gold-tree, my daughter, to eat, I shall be well."

Now it happened about this time that the son of a great king had come from abroad to ask Gold-tree to marry him. The king now agreed to this, and they went abroad. He then went and sent his lads to the hunting hill for a he-goat, and he gave its heart and its liver to his wife to eat, and she rose well and healthy again.

A year after this Silver-tree went to the glen, where there was the well in which there was the trout.

"Troutie, pretty little fellow," said she, "am not I the most beautiful queen in the world?"

"Oh! Indeed you are not."

"Who then?"

"Why, Gold-tree, your daughter."

"Oh! Well, it is long since she was living. It is a year since I ate her heart and liver."

"Oh! Indeed she is not dead. She is married to a great prince abroad."

Silver-tree went home, and begged the king to prepare the longship to set sail, and said, "I am going to see dear Gold-tree, for it is so long since I saw her."

The longship was prepared, and they went away. It was Silver-tree herself that was at the helm, and she steered the ship so well that they were not long at all before they arrived.

The prince was out hunting on the hills. Gold-tree recognized the longship of her father coming.

"Oh!" said she to the servants. "My mother is coming, and she will kill me."

"She shall not kill you at all; we will lock you in a room where she cannot get near you."

This is how it was done; and when Silver-tree came ashore, she began to cry out, "Come to meet your own mother, when she comes to see you."

Gold-tree said that she could not, that she was locked in the room, and that she could not get out of it.

"Will you not put out," said Silver-tree, "your little finger through the keyhole, so that your own mother may give a kiss to it?"

She put out her little finger, and Silver-tree went and put a poisoned stab in it,

and Gold-tree fell dead.

When the prince came home, and found Gold-tree dead, he was in great sorrow, and when he saw how beautiful she was, he did not bury her, but he locked her in a room where nobody would get near her.

In the course of time he married again, and the whole house was under the hand of this wife but one room, and he himself always kept the key of that room. On a certain day of the days he forgot to take the key with him, and the second wife got into the room. What did she see there but the most beautiful woman that she ever saw.

She began to turn and try to wake her, and she noticed the poisoned stab in her finger. She took the stab out, and Gold-tree rose alive, as beautiful as she was ever.

At the fall of night the prince came home from the hunting hill, looking very downcast.

"What gift," said his wife, "would you give me if I could make you laugh?"

"Oh! Indeed, nothing could make me laugh, except

Gold-tree were to come alive again."

"Well, you'll find her alive in the room."

When the prince saw Gold-tree alive he made great rejoicings, and he began to kiss her and kiss her.

Said the second wife to the prince, "Since she is the first one you had, it is better for you to stick to her, and I will go away."

"Oh! Indeed you shall not go away, but I shall have both of you."

At the end of the year, Silver-tree went to the glen, where there was the well, in which there was the trout. "Troutie, pretty little fellow," said she, "am not I the most beautiful queen in the world?"

"Oh! Indeed you are not."

"Who then?"

"Why, Gold-tree, your daughter."

"Oh! Well, she is not alive. It is a year since I put the poisoned stab into her finger."

"Oh! Indeed she is not dead at all."

Silver-tree went home, and begged the king to put the longship in order, for she was going to see her dear Gold-tree, as it was so long since she saw her. The longship was put in order, and they went away. It was Silver-tree herself that was at the helm, and she steered the ship so well that they were not long at all before they arrived.

The prince was out hunting on the hills. Gold-tree knew her father's ship coming.

"Oh!" said she. "My mother is coming, and she will kill me."

"Not at all," said the second wife; "we will go down to meet her."

Silver-tree came ashore. "Come down, Gold-tree, love," said she, "for your own mother has come to you with a precious drink." Of course, the wicked woman had laced it with poison.

"It is a custom in this country," said the second wife, "that the person who offers a drink takes a draught out of it first."

Silver-tree put her mouth to it, and the second wife went and struck it so that some of it went down her throat, and she fell dead. They had only to carry her

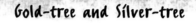

home a dead corpse and bury her.

The prince and his two wives were long alive after this, pleased and peaceful.

I left them there.

BAD BEASTIES

Little Red Riding Hood

By the Brothers Grimm

ONCE UPON A TIME there was a dear little girl who was loved by everyone who looked at her, but most of all by her grandmother, and there was nothing that she would not have given to the child. Once she gave her a little riding hood of red velvet, which suited the little girl so well that she would never wear anything else, so from that day forward she was always called "Little Red Riding Hood."

One day her mother said to her, "Come, Little Red Riding Hood, here is a piece of cake and a bottle of wine, take them to your grandmother. She is ill and weak, and they will do her good. Set out before it gets hot, and when you are going, walk nicely and quietly and do not run off the path, or you may fall and break the bottle; and when you go into her room, don't forget to say, 'Good morning,' and don't peep into every corner before you do it."

"I will take great care," said Little Red Riding Hood to her mother, and gave her hand on it.

The grandmother lived out in the wood, half a league from the village, and just as Little Red Riding Hood entered the wood, a wolf met her. She did not know what a wicked creature he was, and was not at all afraid of him.

"Good day, Little Red Riding Hood," said he.

"Thank you kindly, wolf."

"Where are you going so early, Little Red Riding Hood?"

"To my grandmother's."

"What have you got in your apron?"

"Cake and wine, yesterday was baking day, so poor sick grandmother is to have something good, to make her stronger."

"Where does your grandmother live, Little Red Riding Hood?"

"A good quarter of a league farther on in the wood. Her house stands under the three large oak

trees, the nut trees are just below, you surely must know it," replied Little Red Riding Hood.

The wolf thought to himself, 'What a tender young creature! What a nice plump mouthful! She will be better to eat than the old woman. I must act craftily, so as to catch both.'

So he walked for a short time by the side of Little Red Riding Hood, and then he said, "See, Little Red Riding Hood, how pretty the flowers are about here —why do you not look round? I believe, too, that you do not hear how sweetly the little birds are singing. You walk gravely along as if you were going to school, while everything here in the wood is merry."

Little Red Riding Hood raised her eyes, and when she saw the sunbeams dancing here and there through the trees, and pretty flowers growing everywhere, she thought, 'Suppose I take grandmother a fresh posy? That would please her too. It is so early in the day that I shall still get there in good time.'

So she ran from the path into the wood to look for flowers. And whenever she had picked one, she

fancied that she saw a still prettier one farther on, and ran after it, and so Little Red Riding Hood got deeper and deeper into the wood.

Meanwhile the wolf ran straight to the grandmother's house and knocked at the door.

"Who is there?"

"Little Red Riding Hood," replied the wolf. "She is bringing cake and wine, open the door."

"Lift the latch," called out the grandmother, "I am too weak, and cannot get up."

The wolf lifted the latch, the door sprang open, and without saying a word he went straight to the grandmother's bed and devoured her. Then he put on her clothes, dressed himself in her cap, laid himself in the bed and drew the curtains.

Little Red Riding Hood, however, had been picking flowers, and when she had gathered so many that she could carry no more, she remembered her grandmother, and set out on the way to her.

She was surprised to find the cottage door standing open, and when she went into the room, she had such a strange feeling that she said to herself, "Oh dear! How uneasy I feel today, and at other times I like being with grandmother so much." She called out, "Good morning," but received no answer, so she went to the bed and drew back the curtains. There lay her grandmother with her cap pulled far over her face, and looking very strange.

"Oh, Grandmother," Little Red Riding Hood said, "what big ears you have!"

"All the better to hear you with," was the reply.

"But, Grandmother, what big eyes you have!"

"All the better to see you with."

"But, Grandmother, what large hands you have!"

"All the better to hug you with."

"Oh but, Grandmother, what a terrible big mouth you have!"

"All the better to eat you with!"

And scarcely had the wolf said this, than with one bound he was out of the bed and had swallowed up Little Red Riding Hood.

When the wolf had appeased his appetite, he lay

down again in the bed, fell asleep, and began to snore very loudly.

A huntsman was just passing the house, and thought to himself, 'How the old woman is snoring! I must just see if she wants anything.' So he went into the room, and when he came to the bed, he saw that the wolf was lying in it.

"Do I find you here, you monster!" said he. "I have long sought you!" But just as he was going to fire at him, it occurred to him that the wolf might have devoured the grandmother, and that she might still be saved, so he did not fire, but took a pair of scissors, and began to cut open the stomach of the sleeping wolf.

When the huntsman had made two snips, he saw the little red riding hood shining, and then he made two more snips, and the little girl sprang out, crying, "Ah, how frightened I have been! How dark it was inside the wolf."

After that the aged grandmother came out alive also, but scarcely able to breathe. Little Red Riding Hood, however, quickly fetched great stones with which they filled the wolf's belly, and when he awoke, he wanted to run away, but the stones were so heavy that he collapsed at once, and fell dead.

Then all three were delighted. The huntsman drew off the wolf's skin and went home with it; the grandmother ate the cake and drank the wine which Little Red Riding Hood had brought, and revived. But Little Red Riding Hood thought to herself, 'As long as I live, I will never leave the path by myself to run into the wood, when my mother has forbidden me to do so.'

It is also related that once, when Little Red Riding Hood was again taking cakes to her old grandmother, another wolf spoke to her, and tried to entice her from the path. Little Red Riding Hood, however, was on her guard, and went straight forward on her way. She told her grandmother that she had met the wolf, and that he had said "Good morning" to her, but with such a wicked look in his eyes, that if they had not been on the public road she was certain he would have eaten her up.

"Well," said the grandmother, "we will shut the door, so that he cannot come in."

Soon afterward the wolf knocked, and cried, "Open the door, Grandmother, I am Little Red Riding Hood, and am bringing you some cakes."

But they did not speak, or open the door. So the wolf stole twice or thrice round the house, and at last jumped on the roof, intending to wait until Little

Red Riding Hood went home in the evening, and then to steal after her and devour her in the darkness. But the grandmother saw what was in his thoughts.

In front of the house was a great stone trough, so she said to the child, "Take the pail, Little Red Riding Hood, I made some sausages yesterday, so carry the water in which I boiled them to the trough."

Little Red Riding Hood carried until the great trough was quite full. Then the smell of the sausages reached the wolf, and he sniffed and peeped down, and at last stretched out his neck so far that he could no longer keep his footing and began to slip. He slipped down from the roof straight into the great trough, and was drowned. But Little Red Riding Hood went joyously home, and no one ever did anything to harm her again.

Schippeitaro

From *Tales of Wonder Every Child Should Know*,
by Kate Douglas Wiggin and Nora Archibald Smith

LONG, LONG AGO, in the days of fairies and giants, ogres and dragons, valiant knights, and distressed damsels; in those days, a brave young warrior went out into the wide world in search of adventures.

He traveled over hill and down dale, and for some time he went on without meeting with anything out of the common, but at length, after journeying through a thick forest, he found himself, one evening, on a wild and lonely mountain side. No village was in sight, no cottage, not even the hut of a charcoal burner, so often to be found on the outskirts of the forest. He had been following a faint and much overgrown path, but at length, even that was lost sight of in the dense undergrowth. Twilight was coming on, and in vain he strove to recover the lost track. Each effort seemed only to entangle him more hopelessly in the briars, thick ferns, and tall grasses that grew thickly on all sides. Faint and weary he stumbled on in the fast gathering darkness, until suddenly he came upon an eerie little temple, deserted and half ruined, but which still contained a shrine. Here at least was shelter from the chilly dews and, though the sinister appearance of the temple made the hairs stand up on the back of his neck, here he resolved to pass the night. Food he had none, but, wrapped in his thick mantle, and with his good sword by his side, he lay down, and was soon fast asleep.

Toward midnight he was awakened by a dreadful noise. At first he thought it must be a dream, but the rumpus continued, the whole place resounding with the most terrible shrieks and yells. The young warrior raised himself cautiously, and seizing his sword, peeped quietly through a hole in the ruined wall. He beheld a strange and awful sight. A troop of hideous cats were engaged in a wild and horrible dance, their yells and howling meanwhile echoing through the night. Mingled with their unearthly cries the young warrior could clearly distinguish the words:

"Tell it not to Schippeitaro! Listen for his bark!

Tell it not to Schippeitaro! Keep it close and dark!"

A beautiful, clear full moon shed its light upon this

gruesome scene, which the bold young warrior watched with amazement and horror. Suddenly, the midnight hour being passed, the phantom cats disappeared, and all was silent once more.

The rest of the night passed undisturbed, and the young warrior slept soundly until morning. When he awoke the sun was already up, and he hastened to leave the strange scene of last night's adventure. By the bright morning light he presently discovered traces of a path which the evening before had been invisible. This he followed, and found to his great joy, that it led, not as he had feared, to the forest through which he had come the day before, but in the opposite direction, toward an open plain. There he saw one or two scattered cottages, and, a little farther on, a village.

Pressed by an awful hunger that was gnawing away at his stomach, he was making the best of his way toward the village, when he heard the tones of a woman's voice loud in wailing and pleading. No sooner did these sounds of distress reach the warrior's ears, than his hunger was forgotten, and he hurried on to the nearest cottage, to find out what was the matter and if he could give any help. The people listened to his questions, and shaking their heads sorrowfully, told him that all help was in vain. "Every year," said they, "the mountain spirit claims a victim. The time has come, and this very night will he devour our loveliest maiden. This is the cause of all our weeping and gnashing of teeth." And when the young warrior, filled with wonder, enquired further, they told him that at sunset the victim would be put into a chest, carried to that very ruined temple where he had passed the night, and there left alone. In the morning she would have vanished. So it was each year, and so it would be now; there was no help for it.

The young warrior had a noble heart, and as he listened he was filled with an earnest desire to deliver the maiden. And, the mention of the ruined temple having brought back to his mind the adventure of the night before, he asked the people whether they had ever heard the name of Schippeitaro, and who and what he was. "Schippeitaro is a strong and beautiful dog," was the reply. "He belongs to the head man of our prince who lives only a little way from here. We often see him following his master, he is a fine and brave fellow."

The young knight did not stop to ask more questions, but hurried off to Schippeitaro's master and begged him to lend his dog for one night. The dog's master listened carefully to the warrior's strange tale, but at first was unwilling to agree to his request. At length, however, he agreed to lend Schippeitaro on condition that he should be brought back the next day. Overjoyed, the young warrior led the dog away.

Next he went to see the parents of the unhappy maiden who was to be left out for the sacrifice. The warrior told them to keep their daughter safely in the house and watch her carefully until his return. He then placed the dog Schippeitaro in the chest that had been prepared for the maiden, and, with the help of some of the young men of the village, carried it to the ruined temple, and there set it down. The young men refused to stay one moment on that haunted spot, but hurried down the mountain as if the whole troop of hobgoblins had been at their heels. The young warrior, with no companion but the dog, remained to see what would happen.

The valiant knight waited alone in the dark and the cold, peering into the shadows, alert for any snap of twig or rustle of undergrowth to alert him to an approach. He waited, watched and listened, listened, watched and waited, until at midnight, when the full moon was high in the heaven, and shed her light over the mountain, the phantom cats came once more. This time they had in their midst a huge, black tom-cat, fiercer and more terrible than all the rest, which the young warrior had no difficulty in knowing as the frightful mountain fiend himself. No sooner did this monster catch sight of the chest than he danced and sprang around it, with yells of triumph and hideous joy, followed by his companions. When he had long enough jeered at and taunted his victim, he threw open the top of the chest.

But this time he met his match. The brave
Schippeitaro sprang upon him, and seizing him with
his teeth, held him fast, while the young warrior with
one stroke of his good sword laid the monster dead
at his feet. As for the other cats, too much astonished
to fly, they stood gazing at the dead body of their
leader, and were made short work of by the knight
and Schippeitaro. The young warrior brought back
the brave dog to his master, with a thousand thanks,
told the father and mother of the maiden that their
daughter was free, and the people of the village that
the fiend had claimed his last victim and would
trouble them no more. "You owe all this to the brave
Schippeitaro," he said as he bade them farewell, and
went his way in search of fresh adventures.

Mr Fox

From Joseph Jacobs' *English Fairy Tales*

LADY MARY WAS YOUNG, and Lady Mary was fair. She had two brothers, and more lovers than she could count. But of them all, the bravest and most gallant, was a Mr Fox, whom she met when she was down at her father's country house. No one knew who Mr Fox was; but he was certainly brave, and surely rich, and of all her lovers, Lady Mary cared for him alone. At last it was agreed upon between them that they should be married. Lady Mary asked Mr Fox where they should live, and he described to her his castle, and where it was; but, strange to say, did not ask her, nor her brothers, nor her friends, to come and see it.

So one day, near the wedding day, when her brothers were out, and Mr Fox was away for a day or two on business, as he said, Lady Mary set out for Mr Fox's castle. She journeyed up into the foothills of towering mountains, and after many searchings among crevices and crags, she came at last to it, and a fine strong house it was, with towering, thick walls and a deep moat. And when she came up to the gateway she saw written on it:

Be Bold, Be Bold.

But as the gate was open, she went through it, and found no one there. So she went up to the doorway, and over it she found written:

Be Bold, Be Bold, But Not Too Bold.

Still she went on, till she came into the hall, and

went up the broad stairs till she came to a door in the gallery, over which was written:

Be Bold, Be Bold, But Not Too Bold, Lest That Your Heart's Blood Should Run Cold.

But Lady Mary was a brave one, and she opened the door, and what do you think she saw? Why, bodies and skeletons of beautiful young ladies all stained with blood. So Lady Mary thought it was high time to get out of that horrid place, and she closed the door, went through the gallery, and was just going down the stairs and out of the hall, when who should she see through the window, but Mr Fox dragging a beautiful young lady along from the gateway to the door. Lady Mary rushed downstairs, and hid herself behind a cask, just in time, as Mr Fox came in with the poor young lady who seemed to have fainted. Just as he got near Lady Mary, Mr Fox saw a diamond ring glittering on the finger of the young lady he was dragging, and he tried to pull it

off. But it was tightly fixed, and would not come off, so Mr Fox cursed and swore, and drew his sword, raised it, and brought it down upon the hand of the poor lady. The sword cut off the hand, which fell of all places in the world into Lady Mary's lap. Imagine her horror! But somehow she managed not to jump or shriek—she didn't move so much as an inch or let out so much as a gasp. Mr Fox looked about a bit for the hand, but did not think of looking behind the cask, so at last he went on dragging the young lady up the stairs into the Bloody Chamber.

As soon as she heard him pass through the gallery, Lady Mary crept out of the door, down through the gateway, and ran home as fast as she could.

Now it happened that the very next day the marriage contract of Lady Mary and Mr Fox was to be signed, and there was a splendid breakfast before that with their families and all their friends. And when Mr Fox was seated at the table opposite Lady Mary, he looked at her. "How pale you are this morning, my dear," he soothed.

"Yes," said she, "I had a bad night's rest last night. I had horrible dreams."

"Dreams always mean the opposite of what they seem," said Mr Fox. "But tell us your dream, and I shall do my best to interpret. Whether I can or not, your sweet voice will make the time pass till the happy hour comes."

"I dreamed," said Lady Mary, "that I went yesterday morning to your castle, and I found it in the woods, with high walls, and a deep moat, and over the gateway was written: *Be Bold, Be Bold.*"

"But it is not so, nor it was not so," said Mr Fox.

"And when I came to the doorway over it was written: *Be Bold, Be Bold, But Not Too Bold.*"

"It is not so, nor it was not so," said Mr Fox.

"And then I went upstairs, and came to a gallery, at the end of which was a door, over which was written: *Be Bold, Be Bold, But Not Too Bold, Lest That Your Heart's Blood Should Run Cold.*"

"It is not so, nor it was not so," said Mr Fox.

"And then—and then I opened the door, and the

room was filled with bodies and skeletons of poor dead women, all stained with their blood."

"It is not so, nor it was not so. And God forbid it should be so," said Mr Fox.

"I then dreamed that I rushed down the gallery, and just as I was going down the stairs, I saw you, Mr Fox, coming up to the hall door, dragging after you a poor young lady, rich and beautiful."

"It is not so, nor it was not so. And God forbid it should be so," said Mr Fox.

"I rushed downstairs, just in time to hide myself behind a cask, when you, Mr Fox, came in dragging the young lady by the arm. And, as you passed me, I thought I saw you try and get off her diamond ring, and when you could not, Mr Fox, it seemed to me in my dream, that you cut off the poor lady's hand to get the ring."

"It is not so, nor it was not so. And God forbid it should be so," said Mr Fox, and he was going to say something else as he rose from his seat, when Lady Mary cried out, "But it is so, and it was so.

Here's the hand and ring I have to show." She pulled out the lady's hand from her dress, and pointed it straight at Mr Fox.

At once her brothers and her friends drew their swords and cut Mr Fox into a thousand pieces.

The Farmer and the Badger

From *Japanese Fairy Tales* by Yei Theodora Ozaki

L ONG, LONG AGO in the distant country of Japan, there lived an old farmer and his wife who had made their home in the mountains, far from any town. Their only neighbor was a bad and malicious badger. This badger used to come out every night, whether moonlit or dark, and run across to the farmer's field and spoil the vegetables and the rice that the farmer spent his time carefully cultivating. The badger at last grew so ruthless in his mischievous work, and did so much harm everywhere on the farm, that the good-natured farmer could not stand it any

longer, and determined to put a stop to it. So he lay
in wait day after day and night after night, hoping to
catch the badger, but all in vain. Then he laid traps
for the wicked animal.

The farmer's trouble and patience was rewarded,
for one fine day on going about his rounds he found
the badger caught in a hole he had dug and disguised
for that purpose. The farmer was delighted at having
caught his enemy, and carried him home securely
bound with rope. When he reached the house the
farmer said to his wife, "I have at last caught the bad
badger. You must keep an eye on him while I am out
at work and not let him escape, because I want to get
my revenge on him and have hot badger soup for
supper tonight." Saying this, he hung the badger up to
the rafters of his storehouse and went out to his work
in the fields.

The badger was in great distress, for he did not at
all like the idea of being made into soup that night,
and he thought and thought for a long time, trying to
hit upon some plan by which he might escape. It was

hard to think clearly in his uncomfortable position, for he had been hung upside down. Very near him, at the entrance to the storehouse, looking out toward the green fields and the trees and the pleasant sunshine, stood the farmer's old wife, pounding barley with a huge wooden pestle. She looked tired and old. Her face was seamed with many wrinkles, and was as brown as leather, and every now and then she stopped to wipe the perspiration that rolled down her face. As the badger watched her, a wicked plan formed in his mind.

"Dear lady," said the wily badger, "you must be very weary doing such heavy work in your old age. Won't you let me do that for you? My arms are very strong, and I could relieve you for a little while."

"Thank you for your kindness," said the old woman, "but I cannot let you do this work for me because I must not untie you, for you might escape if I did, and my husband would be very angry if he came home and found you gone."

Now, the badger is one of the most cunning of animals, and he said again in a very sad, gentle voice, "You are very unkind. You might untie me, for I promise not to try to escape. If you are afraid of your husband, I will let you bind me again before his return when I have finished pounding the barley. I am so tired and sore tied up like this. If you would only let me down for just a few minutes I would indeed be very thankful!"

The old woman had a good and simple nature, and could not think badly of anyone. Much less did she think that the badger was only deceiving her in order to get away. She felt sorry, too, for the animal as she turned to look at him. The black-and-white, bristly creature looked in such a sad plight hanging downward from the ceiling by his legs, which were all tied together so tightly that the rope and the knots were cutting into the skin. So in the kindness of her heart, and believing the creature's promise that he would not run away, she untied the rope and let the badger down.

The old woman then gave him the big, heavy pestle and told him to do the work for a short time while she rested. He took the solid piece of wood, but instead of doing the work as he was told, the badger at once sprang upon the old woman and knocked her down with it. He then killed her and cut her up and made soup of her in her own kitchen. But even then the bad badger didn't escape to freedom. Oh no, he was more wicked than that. Instead he stayed and waited for the return of the old farmer.

The old man worked hard in his fields all day, and as he worked he thought with pleasure that no more now would his labor be spoiled by the destructive badger. Toward sunset he left his work and turned to go home. He was very tired, but the thought of the nice supper of hot badger soup awaiting his return cheered him. The thought that the badger might get free and take revenge on the poor old woman never once came into his mind.

He also never imagined that the badger knew magic. But of course, he did. And while the man was tramping home, the badger used his dark arts to take on the old woman's shape. As soon as he saw the old farmer approaching he came out to greet him on the veranda of the little house, saying, "So you have come back at last. I have made the badger soup and have been waiting for you for a long time."

The old farmer quickly took off his straw sandals and sat down before his tiny dinner tray. The innocent man never even dreamed that it was not his

wife but the badger who was waiting upon him, and asked at once for the soup.

Then the badger suddenly transformed himself back to his natural form and cried out, "You wife-eating old man! Look out for the bones in the kitchen!" Laughing loudly and scornfully he escaped out of the house and ran away to his den in the hills.

The old man was left behind alone. He was stunned into silence, and could hardly believe what he had seen and heard. As he realized what must have happened, and the whole truth sunk in, he was so scared and horrified that he fainted right away. After a while he came round and burst into tears. He cried loudly and bitterly. He rocked himself to and fro in his hopeless grief. It seemed too terrible to be real that his faithful old wife had been killed and cooked by the badger while he was working quietly in the fields, knowing nothing of what was going on at home, and congratulating himself on having once and for all got rid of the wicked animal who had so often spoiled his fields. And oh! The horrible thought, he had very nearly drunk the soup that the creature had made of his poor old woman. "Oh dear, oh dear, oh dear!" he wailed aloud, clutching at himself and shaking his head in horror.

Now, not far away there lived in the same mountain a kind, good-natured old rabbit. He heard the old man crying and sobbing and at once set out to see what was the matter, and if there was anything he could do to help his neighbor. The old man told him all that had happened. When the rabbit heard the story he was very angry at the wicked and deceitful badger, and told the old man to leave everything to him and he would avenge his wife's death. The farmer was at last comforted, and, wiping away his tears, thanked the rabbit for his goodness in coming to him in his distress. The rabbit, seeing that the farmer was growing calmer, went back to his home to lay his plans for the punishment of the badger—for he was also very wise, as well as kind.

The next day the weather was fine, and the rabbit went out to find the badger. The evil creature was not to be seen in the woods or on the hillside or in the fields anywhere, so the rabbit went to his den and found the badger hiding there. Despite his dark magic powers, the animal had been afraid to show himself ever since he had escaped from the farmer's house, for fear of the old man's wrath.

The rabbit called out, "Why are you not out on such a beautiful day? Come out with me, and we will go and cut grass on the hills together."

The badger, never doubting that the gentle rabbit was his friend, willingly consented to go out with him, only too glad to get away from the neighborhood of the farmer and the fear of meeting him or being trapped once again. The rabbit led the way miles from their homes, out on the hills where the grass grew tall and thick and sweet. They both set to work to cut down as much as they could carry home, to store it up for their winter's food. When they had each cut down all they wanted they tied it in bundles and then started homeward, each carrying his bundle of grass on his back. This time the rabbit made the badger go first.

When they had gone a little way the rabbit took out a flint and steel, and, striking it over the badger's back as he stepped along in front, set his bundle of grass on fire. The badger heard the flint striking, and asked, "What is that noise, 'Crack, crack'?"

"Oh, that is nothing," replied the rabbit; "I only said 'Crack, crack' because this mountain is called Crackling Mountain."

The Farmer and the Badger

The fire soon spread in the bundle of dry grass on the badger's back. The badger, hearing the crackle of the burning grass asked, "What is that?"

"Now we have come to the Burning Mountain," answered the rabbit.

By this time the bundle was nearly burned out and all the hair had been burned off the badger's back. He now knew what had happened by the smell of the smoke of the burning grass. Screaming with pain the badger ran as fast as he could to his hole.

The rabbit followed and found him lying on his bed groaning with pain.

"What an unlucky fellow you are!" said the rabbit. "I can't imagine how this happened! I will bring you some medicine that will heal your back quickly!"

The rabbit went away glad and smiling to think that the punishment upon the badger had already begun. He hoped that the badger would die of his burns, for he felt that nothing could be too bad for the animal, who was guilty of murdering a poor, helpless old woman who had trusted him. He went home and made an ointment by mixing some sauce and red pepper together.

He carried this to the badger, but before putting it on he told him that it would cause him great pain, but that he must bear it patiently, because it was a wonderful medicine for burns and scalds and such wounds. The badger thanked him and begged him to apply it at once. But no language can describe the agony of the badger as soon as the red pepper had been pasted all over his sore back. He rolled over and over and howled loudly. The rabbit, looking on, felt that the farmer's wife was beginning to be avenged.

The badger was in bed for about a month, but at last, in spite of the red pepper application, his burns healed and he got well. When the rabbit saw that the badger was getting well, he thought of another plan by which he could compass the creature's death. So he went one day to pay the badger a visit and to congratulate him on his recovery. During the conversation the rabbit mentioned that he was going fishing, and described how pleasant fishing was when the weather was fine and the sea smooth.

The badger listened with pleasure to the rabbit's account of the way he passed his time now, and forgot all his pains and his month's illness, and thought what fun it would be if he could go fishing too, so he asked the rabbit if he would take him the next time he went out to fish. This was just what the rabbit wanted, so he agreed.

Then he went home and built two boats, one of wood and the other of clay. At last they were both finished, and as the rabbit stood and looked at his work he felt that all his trouble would be well rewarded if his plan succeeded, and he could manage to kill the wicked badger now.

The day came when the rabbit had arranged to take the badger fishing. He kept the wooden boat himself and gave the badger the clay boat. The badger, who knew nothing about boats, was delighted with his new boat and thought how kind it was of the rabbit to give it to him. They both got into their boats and set out. After going some distance from the

shore the rabbit proposed that they should try their boats and see which one could go the quickest. The badger fell in with the proposal, and they both set to work to row as fast as they could for some time. In

the middle of the race the badger found his boat
going to pieces, for the water now began to soften the
clay. He cried out in great fear to the rabbit to help
him. But the rabbit answered that he was avenging the
old woman's murder, and that this had been his
intention all along, and that he was happy to think
that the badger had at last met his deserts for all his
evil crimes, and was to drown with no one to help
him. Then he raised his oar and struck at the badger
with all his strength till he fell with the sinking clay
boat and was seen no more.

Thus at last he kept his promise to the old farmer.
The rabbit now turned and rowed shoreward, and
having landed and pulled his boat upon the beach,
hurried back to tell the old farmer everything, and
how the badger, his enemy, had been killed.

The old farmer thanked him with tears in his eyes.
He said that till now he could never sleep at night or
be at peace in the daytime, thinking of how his wife's
death was unavenged, but from this time he would be
able to sleep and eat as of old. He begged the rabbit

to stay with him and share his home, so from this day the rabbit went to stay with the old farmer and they both lived together as good friends to the end of their days.

Boots and the Troll

From *Popular Tales from the Norse*,
by Sir George Webbe Dasent

ONCE ON A TIME there was a poor man who had
three sons. When he and his wife died, the two
elder sons set off into the world to try their luck, but
the youngest boy they wouldn't have with them at any
price. "As for you," they said, "you're fit for nothing
but to sit and poke about in the ashes of the fire in
the kitchen." So the two went off and managed to
find jobs at the palace—one lad went to work for the
coachman and the other went to work for the
gardener. But the youngest boy, whom all called
Boots, he set off too, and took with him a great,

long, bread kneading-trough, which was the only
thing his parents left behind them, but which the
other two would not bother themselves with. It was
heavy to carry, but it was the only thing he had to
remind him of his parents, so he did not like to leave
it behind. Boots carried the great, long, bread
kneading-trough on his back, and after he had
trudged a bit, he too came to the palace, and asked
for a job. The servants in each department told him
they did not need him, but he begged so persuasively
that at last he got leave to work in the kitchen, and
carry in wood and water for the kitchen maid. He
was quick and ready, and in a little while everyone
liked him; but the two others were dull, and so they
got more kicks than money, and grew quite envious
of Boots, when they saw how much better he got on.

Just opposite the palace, across a lake, lived a troll,
who had seven silver ducks that swam on the lake, so
that they could be seen from the palace. The king had
often longed for these, and so, to stir up trouble, the
two elder brothers told the coachman, "If our

brother only wanted to, he has said he could easily get the king those seven silver ducks."

You may fancy it wasn't long before the coachman told this to the king, so the king called Boots before him, and said, "Your brothers say you can get me the silver ducks, so now go and fetch them."

"I'm sure I never said anything of the kind," said the Boots, astonished—and not a little bit alarmed.

"You did say so, and you shall fetch them," insisted the king, who would not take no for an answer.

"Well! Well!" said the boy. "Needs must, I suppose, but give me a bushel of rye, and a bushel of wheat, and I'll see what I can do."

So the boy was given the bushel of rye and the bushel of wheat, and he put them into the kneading-trough he had brought with him from home, got into it, and rowed across the lake. When he reached the other side he began to walk along the shore, and to sprinkle and scatter the grain, and at last he coaxed the ducks into his kneading-trough, and rowed back as fast as he could.

When he got half across, the troll came out of his house, and set eyes on him.

"HALLOA!" roared out the troll. "Is it you that has gone off with my seven silver ducks?"

"AYE! AYE!" said the boy.

"Then just you wait till I get my hands on you!" roared the troll.

Of course, when Boots got back to the king, with the seven silver ducks, he was more liked than ever, and even the king was pleased to say, "Well done!"

But at this his brothers grew more and more spiteful and envious, and they went and told the coachman that their brother had said, that if he wanted to, he was man enough to get the king the troll's bed quilt, which had a gold patch and a silver patch, and a silver patch and a gold patch. Once again, the coachman was not slow in telling all this to the king. So the king said to the boy how his brothers had said he could steal the troll's bed quilt, with gold and silver patches, so now he must go and do it, or lose his life.

Boots answered that he had never thought or said any such thing, but when he found there was no help for it, he begged the king for three days to think over the matter.

So when the three days were gone, he rowed over in his kneading-trough, and went spying. At last he saw those in the troll's cave come out and hang the quilt out to air, and as soon as ever they had gone back into the face of the rock, Boots pulled the quilt down, and rowed away with it as fast as he could.

And when he was half across, out came the troll and set eyes on him, and roared out, "HALLOA! Is it you who went off with my seven silver ducks?"

"AYE! AYE!" said the lad.

"And now, have you taken my bed quilt, with a silver patch and a gold patch, and a gold patch and a silver patch?"

"AYE! AYE!" said the boy.

"Then just you wait till I get my hands on you!" bellowed the troll.

But when Boots got back with the gold and silver patchwork quilt, everyone was fonder of him than ever, and he was made the king's close servant.

At this, the other two were still more vexed, and, to be revenged, they went and told the coachman, "Now, our brother has said that if he wants, he is man enough to get the king the gold harp that the troll has, and that harp is of such a kind, that all who listen when it is played grow glad, however sad they may be."

Yes! The coachman went and told the king, and

this time he said to the boy, "If you have said this, you shall do it. If you do it, you shall have the princess and half the kingdom. If you don't, you shall lose your life."

"I'm sure I never thought or said anything of the kind," the boy answered, "but if there's no help for it, I may as well try. ButI must have six days to think about it."

Yes! He might have six days, but when they were over, he must set out.

Then he took a long iron nail, a birch wood pin and a waxen candle end in his pocket, and rowed across, and walked up and down before the troll's cave, looking stealthily about him. So when the troll came out, he saw him at once, for Boots was right in front of him.

"HO, HO!" roared the troll. "Is it you who took my seven silver ducks?"

"AYE! AYE!" said the boy.

"And it is you who took my bed quilt, with the gold and silver patches?" asked the troll.

"AYE! AYE!" said the lad.

So the troll caught hold of him at once, and took him off into the cave in the face of the rock.

"Now, daughter dear," said the troll, "I've caught the fellow who stole the silver ducks and my bed quilt with gold and silver patches. Put him into the

fattening coop and feed him up, and when he's fat, we'll kill him, and make a feast for our friends."

The troll's daughter was willing enough, and put him at once into the fattening coop, and there he stayed eight days, fed on the best, both in meat and drink, and as much as he could cram.

So, when the eight days were over, the troll said to his daughter to go down and cut him in his little finger, that they might see if he were fat.

Down she came to the coop. "Out with your little finger!" she said.

But Boots stuck out his long iron nail, and she cut at it.

"Nay! Nay! He's as hard as iron still," said the troll's daughter, when she got back to her father. "We can't cook him yet."

After another eight days the same thing happened, and this time Boots stuck out his birch wood pin.

"He's a little better," she said, when she got back to the troll; "but he'll be as hard as wood to chew."

When another eight days were gone, the troll told

his daughter to go down and see if he wasn't fat now.

"Out with your little finger," said the troll's daughter, when she reached the coop, and this time Boots stuck out the waxen candle end.

"Now he'll do nicely," she said.

"Will he?" said the troll. "Well, then, I'll just set off and ask the guests. Meantime you must kill him, and roast half and boil half."

So when the troll had been gone a little while, the daughter began to sharpen a great long knife.

"Is that what you're going to kill me with?" asked the boy.

"Yes it is," said she.

"But it isn't sharp," said the lad. "Just let me sharpen it for you, and then you'll find it easier work to kill me."

So she let him have the knife, and he began to rub and sharpen it on the whetstone.

"Just let me try it on one of your hair plaits, I think it's about right now," said Boots at last.

And he got leave to do that, but at the same time

BAD BEASTIES

that he grasped the plait of hair, he pulled back her head, which he cut off swiftly. Then half of her he roasted and half he boiled, and served it all up.

After that he dressed himself in her clothes, and sat in the corner.

So when the troll ariived back at home with his guests, he called out to his daughter—for he thought all the time it was his daughter—to come and take a something to eat.

"No, thank you," said the lad, "I don't care for food, I'm so sad and downcast."

"Oh!" said the troll. "If that's all, you know the cure, take the harp and play a tune on it."

"Yes," said the boy, "But where has it got to? I can't find it."

"Why, you know well enough, as you used it last," the troll answered. "Where should it be but over the door yonder?"

The boy did not wait to be told twice. He took down the harp, and went in and out of the cave playing tunes. Then he quickly jumped into the kneading-trough and rowed off, so that the foam flew around him.

After a while the troll thought his daughter was a long while gone, and went out to see what ailed her. Then he saw the boy in the kneading-trough, far, far out on the lake.

"HALLOA! Is it you," he roared, "that took my seven silver ducks?"

"AYE, AYE!" said the boy.

"Is it you that took my bed quilt with the gold and silver patches?"

"Yes!" said the boy.

"And now you have taken off my gold harp?" screamed the troll.

"Yes I have!" said the boy. "I've got it with me, sure enough."

"And haven't I eaten you up after all, then?"

"No, no! 'Twas your own daughter you ate," answered the lad.

But when the troll heard this news, he was so angry he burst, and then Boots decided to row back, and took a whole heap of gold and silver with him, as much as the trough could carry. And so when he came back to the palace with the gold harp, he got the princess and half the kingdom, exactly as the king had promised him. And as for his elder brothers,

Boots treated them well enough, for he thought that they had only wished him good when they said what they had said.

the Bunyip

From Andrew Lang's *Brown Fairy Book*

ONG, LONG AGO, far, far away on the other side
of the world, some young men left the camp
where they lived to get some food for their wives and
children. The sun was hot, but they liked heat, and as
they went they ran races and tried to see who could
hurl his spear the farthest, or was cleverest in
throwing a strange weapon called a boomerang, which
always returns to the thrower. They did not get on
very fast at this rate, but presently they reached a flat
place that in time of flood was full of water, but was
now, in the height of summer, only a set of pools,

each surrounded with a fringe of plants, with bulrushes standing in the inside of all. In that country the people are fond of eating the roots of bulrushes, which they think as good as onions, and one of the young men said that they had better collect some of the roots and carry them back to the camp. It did not take them long to weave the tops of the willows into a basket, and they were just going to wade into the water and pull up the bulrush roots when a youth suddenly called out, "Why should we waste our time in foraging and gathering, doing work that is only fit for women and children? Let them come and get the roots for themselves. We will fish for eels and catch anything else we can get."

This delighted the rest of the party, and they all began to arrange their fishing lines, made from the bark of the yellow mimosa, and to search for bait for their hooks. Most of them used worms, but one man, who had put a piece of raw meat for dinner into his skin wallet, cut off a little bit and baited his line with it, unseen by his companions.

For a long time they cast patiently, without receiving a single bite. The sun had grown low in the sky, and it seemed as if they would have to go home empty-handed, not even with a basket of roots to show, when the youth who had baited his hook with raw meat suddenly saw his line disappear under the water. Something—a very big fish he supposed—was pulling so hard that he could hardly keep his feet, and for a few minutes it seemed either as if he must let go or be dragged into the pool. He cried to his friends to help him, and at last, trembling with fright at what they were going to see, they managed between them to land on the bank a creature that was neither a calf nor a seal, but something of both, with a long, broad tail. They looked at each other with horror, cold shivers running down their spines; for though they had never beheld it, there was not a man amongst them who did not know what it was—the cub of the awful Bunyip! Now the Bunyip was thought to be a wicked creature that lurked in dank, watery places, and went out at night to prey on women and children

The Bunyip

and devour them. It was said that it knew terrible magic and would use all means, fair and foul, to defend itself, its evil home, and—of course—its offspring!

As the young men stared at the monstrous cub in dread, all of a sudden the silence was broken by a low wail, answered by another from the other side of the pool, as the enraged Bunyip mother rose up from her den, her horrible yellow eyes glinting in the darkness. "Let it go! Let it go!" whispered the men to each other, but the captor declared that he had caught it, and was going to keep it. He had promised his sweetheart, he said, that he would bring back enough meat for her father's house to feast on for three days, and though they would not eat the little Bunyip, her brothers and sisters should have it to play with. So he threw the little Bunyip onto his shoulders, and set out for the camp, never heeding the mother's cries of distress as she hunted for her baby in vain.

By this time it was getting near sunset, and the plain was in shadow, though the tops of the

mountains were still quite bright. The youths had all
ceased to be afraid, when they were startled by a low
rushing sound behind them, and, looking round, saw
that the pool was slowly rising, and the spot where
they had landed the Bunyip cub was quite covered.
"What could it be?" they asked one another; there
was not a cloud in the sky, yet the water had risen
higher already than they had ever known it do before.
For an instant they stood watching as if they were
frozen, then they turned and ran with all their might,
the man with the Bunyip baby running faster than all.
When he reached a high peak overlooking all the
plain he stopped to take breath and turned to see if
he was safe yet.

Safe! Why only the tops of the trees remained
above that sea of water, and these were fast
disappearing. They must run swifter than the wind
itself if they were to escape. So on they flew, scarcely
feeling the ground as they went, till they flung
themselves on the ground before the holes scooped
out of the earth where they had all been born. In the

village, the old men were sitting in front, the children were playing, and the women chattering together, when the little Bunyip cub was flung into their midst, and there was scarcely a child among them who did not know that something terrible was upon them. "The water! The water!" gasped one of the young men, and there it was, slowly but steadily mounting the ridge itself.

Parents and children clung together, as if by that means they could drive back the advancing flood, and the youth who had caused all this terrible catastrophe, seized his sweetheart, and cried, "I will climb with you to the top of that tree, and there no waters can reach us." But, as he spoke, something cold touched him, and quickly he glanced down at his feet. Then with a shudder he saw that they were feet no longer, but bird's claws. He looked at the girl he was clasping, and beheld a great black bird standing at his side, he turned to his friends, but a flock of great, awkward flapping creatures stood in their place. He put his hands to cover his face, but

they were no more hands, only the ends of wings,
and when he tried to speak, a noise such as he had
never heard before seemed to come from his throat,
which had suddenly become narrow and slender.
Already the water had risen to his waist, and he
found himself sitting easily upon it, while its surface
reflected the image of a black swan, one of many.

Never again did the swans become men, but they
are still different from other swans, for in the
nighttime those who listen can hear them talk in a
language that is certainly not swan's language, and
there are even sounds of laughing and talking, unlike
any noise made by the swans whom we know.

The little Bunyip was carried home by its mother,
and after that the waters sank back to their own
channels. The side of the pool where she lives is
always shunned by everyone, as nobody knows when
she may suddenly put out her head and draw him
into her mighty jaws. But people say that underneath
the black waters of the pool she has a house filled
with beautiful things, such as mortals who dwell on

the earth have no idea of. Though how they know I cannot tell you, as nobody has ever seen it.

Beauty and the Beast

From *Europa's Fairy Tales*, Joseph Jacobs

THERE WAS ONCE a merchant who had three daughters, and he loved them better than life itself. Now it happened that he had to travel on a long journey to buy some goods, and when he was just starting he said to them, "What shall I bring you back, my dears? Name any gift you like and it shall be yours."

And the eldest daughter asked to have a necklace, and the second daughter wished to have a gold chain, but the youngest daughter said, "Bring back yourself, Papa, and that is what I want the most."

"Nonsense, child," said her father, "you must say something that I may remember to bring back for you. Surely there is something you wish for?"

"So," she said, "then bring me back a rose, Father."

Well, the merchant went on his journey and did his business in distant lands and bought a pearl necklace for his eldest daughter, and a gold chain for his second daughter, but he knew it was no use getting a rose for the youngest while he was so far away because it would fade and die before he got home. So he made up his mind he would get a rose for her the day he got near his house, so it stayed perfect for his beloved daughter.

When all his merchanting was done he rode off home and forgot all about finding a rose till he was almost home. Then he suddenly remembered what he had promised his youngest daughter, and looked about to see if he could find a beautiful bloom. Near where he had stopped he saw a great garden, and getting off his horse he wandered about in it till he found a lovely rose bush, and he plucked the most beautiful rose he could see on it. At that moment he heard a sudden crash like thunder, and looking around he saw a huge monster, with two tusks sticking out from its mouth, and fiery eyes surrounded by bristles, and horns coming out of its head and spreading over its back.

"Mortal," said the Beast, "who told you that you might pluck my roses?"

"Please, sir," said the merchant in fear and terror for his life, "I promised my daughter to bring her home a rose and forgot about it till the last moment, and then I saw your beautiful garden and thought you would not miss a single rose, or else I would have asked your permission."

"Thieving is thieving," said the Beast, "whether it be a rose or a diamond. You must pay with your life."

The merchant fell on his knees and begged for his life for the sake of his three daughters who had none but him to work and support them.

"Well, mortal, well," said the Beast, "I grant your life on one condition—and one condition only: seven days from now you must bring this youngest daughter of yours, for whose sake you have broken into my garden and committed this crime, and leave her here in your place. Otherwise, swear that you will return and that you yourself will become my servant."

So the merchant made his promise by swearing

solemnly and, taking his rose, mounted his horse. As he rode home, his heart was as heavy as lead, his mind full of woe.

As soon as he got into his house his daughters came rushing round him, clapping their hands and showing their joy in every way. The merchant tried hard not to show his anxiety and sorrow, and soon he gave the necklace to his eldest daughter, and the chain to his second daughter. But when he gave the rose to his youngest, a deep sigh escaped his lips.

"Oh, thank you, Father," they all cried.

But the youngest said, "Why did you sigh so deeply when you gave me my rose?"

"Later on I will tell you," said the merchant, his eyes full of dread.

So for several days the family got on with everyday life as normal, though the merchant wandered about gloomy and sad, and nothing his daughters could do would cheer him up till at last he took his youngest daughter aside and said to her, "Bella, do you love your father?"

"Of course I do, Father, of course I do," the maiden replied.

"Well, now I have to ask that you do something because you love me—and it may well be the hardest thing that I ever have to ask of you," explained the merchant. And then he told her of all that had occurred with the Beast when he got the rose for her.

Bella was very upset, as you can well think, and then she said, "Oh, Father, it was all on account of me that you fell into the power of this Beast, so I will go with you to him. Perhaps he will do me no harm, but even if he does, better harm to me than evil to my dear father."

So next day the merchant took Bella behind him on his horse, as was the custom in those days, and they plodded off, hanging their heads, to the dwelling of the Beast. They allowed the horse to go as slowly as he liked, but the time finally came when they at last arrived. The merchant and his daughter alighted from the horse to find that the doors of the house swung open on their own! And what do you think they saw

there? Nothing. So they nervously went up the broad,
stone steps and went through the great entrance hall,
and went into the grand dining room, and there they
saw a table spread with all manner of beautiful glasses
and plates and dishes and cutlery, with plenty to eat
upon it. So they waited and they waited, thinking that
the owner of the house would appear, till at last the
merchant said, "Let's sit down and see what will
happen then." And when they sat down invisible
hands passed them things to eat and to drink, and
they ate and drank to their heart's content. And when
they arose from the table it arose too and disappeared
through the door as if it were being carried by
invisible servants.

Suddenly there appeared before them the Beast,
who said to the merchant, "Is this your youngest
daughter?" And when he was told that it was, he said,
"Is she willing to stop here with me?" And then he
looked at Bella who said, in a trembling voice,

"Yes, sir."

"Well, no harm shall befall you," replied the Beast,

BAD BEASTIES

and Bella thought that she saw a kind light in his beastly eyes.

With that, he led the merchant down to his horse and told him he might come on the same day the following week to visit his daughter. Then the Beast returned to Bella and said to her, "This house, with everything in it, is yours. If you want anything at all, just clap your hands and ask for it, and it will be brought to you." And with that he made a sort of bow and went away.

So Bella lived on in the Beast's home of splendor and finery, and was waited on by invisible servants, and had whatever she liked to eat and to drink. The next day, when the Beast came to her, though he looked so terrible, she had been so well treated that she had lost a great deal of her fear of him. So they spoke together about the gorgeous garden—which was quite the most beautiful she had ever seen or imagined—and about the house and about her father's business and about all manner of things, so that Bella lost altogether her dread of the Beast.

BAD BEASTIES

Before Bella knew it, a week had flown by, and her
father came to see her. He found her quite happy, and
he felt much less worry of her fate at the hands of
the Beast. So it went on, Bella seeing and talking to
the Beast every day, till she got to quite like him.

One day the Beast did not come at his usual time,
just after the midday meal, and Bella missed him
awfully. She searched all over the house, but could
find no sign of him at all. So she wandered about the
garden trying to find him, calling out his name, but
received no reply. Bella's heart began to race with
anxiety. Then at last she came to the rose bush from
which her father had plucked the rose, and there,
under it, what do you think she saw! There was
the Beast lying, huddled up, without any life
or motion. She threw herself down by his
side, dreadfully shocked and
upset, remembering all the
kindness that the Beast
had shown her. She
began to sob, saying,

"Oh, Beast, Beast, why did you die? I was getting to love you so much."

No sooner had she uttered these words than the hide of the Beast split in two and out came the most handsome young prince! He told her that he had been enchanted by a magician and that he could not recover his natural form unless a maiden should, of her own accord, declare that she loved him.

Thereupon the prince sent for the merchant and his daughters, and he was married to Bella, and they all lived happy ever after.

The Goblin Pony

From Andrew Lang's *Grey Fairy Book*

THERE WAS ONCE an old woman named Peggy, whose daughter and husband had died, leaving her to look after her three grandchildren alone. The eldest was a boy who was of the age to want to be out and about by himself, having an eye for the girls. The next grandchild was a daughter, who was kind and hard-working, and helped Peggy to look after the family. The youngest grandchild was a little boy called Richard, of whom Peggy was especially fond.

One particularly cold, dark night, Peggy felt a chill of fear spread through her old bones, and she gave her grandchildren a solemn warning. "Don't stir from the fireplace tonight," she said, "for the wind is blowing so violently that the house shakes. Besides, this is Halloween, when the witches are abroad, and the goblins, who are their servants, are wandering about in all sorts of disguises, doing harm to the children of men."

"Why should I stay here?" said the eldest of the young people. "No, I must go and see what the daughter of old Jacob, the rope-maker, is doing. She wouldn't close her blue eyes all night if I didn't visit her father before the moon had gone down."

"I must go and catch lobsters and crabs," said the granddaughter. "If I don't, I will have nothing to sell at market tomorrow and we will stay hungry at suppertime! Not all the witches and goblins in the world shall hinder me from going out tonight."

So they all determined to go on their business or pleasure, and scorned the wise advice of old Peggy. Only the youngest child hesitated a minute, when she said to him, "You stay here, my little Richard, and I will tell you beautiful stories." But he wanted to pick a bunch of wild thyme and some blackberries by moonlight, and ran out after the others.

When they got outside they said, "The old woman talks of wind and storm, but never was the weather finer or the sky more clear, see how majestically the moon stalks through the transparent clouds!"

Then all of a sudden they noticed a little black pony close beside them, which none of them had heard approach.

"Oh, ho!" they said. "That must be old Farmer Valentine's new pony, perhaps it has escaped from its stable and is going down to drink at the pond."

"My pretty little pony," said the eldest, patting the creature with his hand, "you mustn't run too far. I'll take you to the pond myself."

With these words he jumped on the pony's back. He was quickly followed by his sister, who reached down a hand and helped little Richard swing himself astride, for he didn't like to be left behind.

Off they set to the pond, trotting along in the

moonlight. On the way, they met several of their companions, and they invited them all to mount the pony, which they did, and the little creature did not seem to mind the extra weight, but jogged merrily on.

The quicker it trotted the more the young people enjoyed the fun. They dug their heels into the pony's sides and called out, "Gallop, little pony, you have never had such brave riders on your back before!"

In the meantime the wind had risen again, and the waves began to howl, but the pony did not seem to mind the noise, and instead of going to the pond, cantered gaily toward the seashore.

Richard began to regret not going to gather his thyme and blackberries, and the eldest brother seized the pony by the mane and tried to make it turn around, for he remembered the blue

The Goblin Pony

eyes of Jacob the rope-maker's daughter. But he tugged and pulled in vain, for the pony galloped straight on into the sea, till the waves met its forefeet. As soon as it felt the water it neighed and capered about with glee, advancing quickly into the foaming billows. When the waves had covered the children's legs they repented their careless behavior, and cried out, "The cursed little black pony is bewitched. If we had only listened to old Peggy's advice we shouldn't have been lost."

The further the pony advanced, the higher rose the sea. At last the waves covered the children's heads and they were all drowned.

Toward morning old Peggy went out, for she was anxious about the fate of her grandchildren. She sought them high and low, but could not find them anywhere. She asked all the neighbors if they had seen the children, but no one knew anything about them, except that the eldest had not been with the blue-eyed daughter of Jacob the rope-maker. Indeed, several of them were searching for their own missing girls and boys, who had vanished without trace.

As Peggy was going home, bowed with grief, she saw a little black pony coming toward her, springing and prancing in every direction. When it got quite near her it neighed loudly, and galloped past her so quickly that in a moment it was out of her sight.

The Jelly Fish and the Monkey

From *Japanese Fairy Tales* by Yei Theodora Ozaki

LONG AGO, in old Japan, in the days when the jelly fish was a hard creature with a shell and bones, the oceans were governed by Rin Jin, the Dragon King of the Sea. He was the ruler of all sea creatures both great and small, and lived in a palace at the bottom of the ocean so beautiful that no one has ever seen anything like it, even in dreams. But despite all this, the Dragon King was not happy, for he reigned on his own and was lonely. Finally he decided to find a wife and called several fish ambassadors to search the oceans for a suitable bride.

At length they brought to the palace a lovely young dragon, with scales like the glittering green of the waves and eyes the gleaming white of pearls, whom the king fell in love with at once. The wedding ceremony was celebrated with great splendor and every living thing in the oceans rejoiced, from the hugest whale to the tiniest shrimp.

The Dragon King and his bride were very happy together—for just two months, for then the Dragon Queen suddenly fell very ill. The desperate king ordered the best doctor and nurses to look after her, but instead of getting better, the young queen grew daily worse. The doctor tried to excuse himself by saying that although he knew the right kind of medicine, it was impossible to find it in the sea.

"Tell me what it is!" demanded the Dragon King.

"The liver cut from a live monkey!" answered the doctor. "If we could only get that, Her Majesty would soon recover."

"Well, even though we sea creatures cannot leave the ocean, we MUST get a monkey to cut up somehow," decided the king.

He called his chief steward for advice, who thought for some time, and declared, "I know! The jelly fish is ugly to look at, but he has a hard shell and four bony legs and can walk on land. An island where there are monkeys lies a few hours' swim to the south—let us send the jelly fish there. If he can't catch a monkey, maybe he can trick one into coming here."

The jelly fish was summoned and ordered to entice a monkey to the Dragon King's palace. Although very worried about the task, the poor jelly fish had no choice but to swim off at once. Luckily, when he reached Monkey Island he saw a big pine tree and on one of its branches was just what he was looking for —a live monkey.

"How do you do, Mr Monkey?" called the jelly fish, thinking quickly of a plan. "Isn't it a lovely day?" he added politely.

"A very fine day," answered the monkey. "I have never seen you before. What is your name?"

"My name is Jelly Fish. I have heard so much of

your beautiful island that I have come to see it," answered the jelly fish.

"I am very glad to see you," said the monkey.

"By the bye," said the jelly fish, "have you seen the Palace of the Dragon King of the Sea where I live?"

"I have often heard of it, but I have never seen it!" answered the monkey.

"Then you ought most surely to come. The beauty of the palace is beyond all description—it is certainly the most lovely place in the world," said the jelly fish, and he described the beauty and grandeur of the Sea King's Palace, the wonders of its garden and the oceans all around.

The monkey grew more and more interested, and came down the tree. "I should love to come with you," he sighed, "but how am I to cross the water? I can't swim."

"There is no difficulty about that. I can carry you on my back," said the jelly fish.

So the excited monkey leaped onto the jelly fish's hard shell and the creature plunged into the sea. Thus

they went along, skimming through the waves until
they were about halfway, when the jelly fish began to
feel more and more sorry for the terrible fate that lay
ahead for the monkey. With a sigh, he told the
monkey everything—how he was to be killed for his
liver, to save the Dragon Queen.

The poor monkey was horrified, and very angry at
the trick played upon him. But he was clever, so tried

to keep calm and think of some way to escape.

A bright thought struck him, and he said quite cheerfully, "What a pity it was, Mr Jelly Fish, that you did not tell me before we left the island! I have several livers and would happily have given you one— but I have left them all hanging on the pine tree."

The jelly fish was very disappointed, for he believed the story.

"Never mind," said the monkey, "take me back to where you found me and I will fetch a liver."

The pleased jelly fish turned his course toward Monkey Island once more. But no sooner had he reached the shore than the sly monkey scampered up into the pine tree and jeered at him. "Of course, I won't GIVE you my liver, but come and get it if you can!" mocked the monkey.

There was nothing for the jelly fish to do but return to the Dragon King and confess his failure.

Of course, the Dragon King was beside himself with fury. He ordered a terrible punishment, that all the bones were to be drawn out from the jelly fish's body, that he was to be beaten with sticks until his shell broke off and he was left a flattened pulp, then banished from the palace.

The jelly fish, humiliated and horrified beyond all words, cried out for pardon. But the Dragon King's order had to be obeyed. And that is why, ever since, the descendents of the jelly fish have all been soft and boneless, just as you see them today, thrown up by the waves high upon the shores of Japan.

The Strange Visitor

From Joseph Jacobs' *English Fairy Tales*

A WOMAN WAS SITTING at her reel one night.

And still she sat, and still she reeled, and still she wished for company.

In came a pair of broad broad feet, and sat down at the fireside.

And still she sat, and still she reeled, and still she wished for company.

In came a pair of small small legs, and sat down on the broad broad feet.

And still she sat, and still she reeled, and still she

wished for company.

In came a pair of thick thick knees, and sat down on the small small legs.

And still she sat, and still she reeled, and still she wished for company.

In came a pair of thin thin thighs, and sat down on the thick thick knees.

And still she sat, and still she reeled, and still she wished for company.

In came a pair of huge huge hips, and sat down on the thin thin thighs.

And still she sat, and still she reeled, and still she wished for company.

In came a wee wee waist, and sat down on the huge huge hips.

And still she sat, and still she reeled, and still she wished for company.

In came a pair of broad broad shoulders, and sat down on the wee wee waist.

And still she sat, and still she reeled, and still she wished for company.

In came a pair of small small arms, and sat down on the broad broad shoulders.

And still she sat, and still she reeled, and still she wished for company.

In came a pair of huge huge hands, and sat down on the small small arms.

And still she sat, and still she reeled, and still she wished for company.

In came a small small neck, and sat down on the broad broad shoulders.

And still she sat, and still she reeled, and still she wished for company.

In came a huge huge head, and sat down on the small small neck.

"How did you get such broad broad feet?" asked the woman.

"Much tramping, much tramping." (*gruffly*)

"How did you get such small small legs?"

"Aih-h-h!-late—and wee-e-e—moul." (*whiningly*)

"How did you get such thick thick knees?"

"Much praying, much praying." (*piously*)

"How did you get such thin thin thighs?"

"Aih-h-h!—late—and wee-e-e—moul." (*whiningly*)

"How did you get such huge huge hips?"

"Much sitting, much sitting." (*gruffly*)

"How did you get such a wee wee waist?"

"Aih-h-h!—late—and wee-e-e—moul." (*whiningly*)

"How did you get such broad broad shoulders?"

"With carrying broom, with carrying broom." (*gruffly*)

"How did you get such small small arms?"

"Aih-h-h!—late—and wee-e-e—moul." (*whiningly*)

"How did you get such huge huge hands?"

"Threshing with an iron flail, threshing with an iron flail." (*gruffly*)

"How did you get such a small small neck?"

"Aih-h-h!—late—wee-e-e—moul." (*pitifully*)

"How did you get such a huge huge head?"

"Much knowledge, much knowledge." (*keenly*)

"What do you come for?"

(*At the top of the voice, with a wave of the arm and a stamp of the feet.*) "FOR YOU!"

The Strange Visitor

About the Authors

HANS CHRISTIAN ANDERSEN 1805~1875

Born in Denmark, Hans Christian Andersen was apprenticed to a weaver and a tailor, before working as an actor and singer in Copenhagen. While in the theater he wrote poetry and stories and became famous worldwide for children's tales. These have been translated into over 150 languages, and have inspired movies, animated films, plays, and ballets.

L. FRANK BAUM 1856~1919

Lyman Frank Baum was born in New York, to a wealthy family. As a child he began writing stories, printing them on his own printing press, and later worked as a newspaper and magazine editor. His greatest success was writing *The Wonderful Wizard of Oz*. He went on to write thirteen books about the land of Oz, and many other short stories, poems and scripts.

THOMAS FREDERICK CRANE 1844~1927

American Thomas Frederick Crane worked as a lawyer and academic, but devoted much of his spare time to collecting folklore.

SIR GEORGE WEBBE DASENT 1817~1896

Sir George Webbe Dasent was educated at Oxford University and became a diplomat in Sweden. There he met Jacob Grimm and became interested in folk tales. In England, he worked as assistant editor of *The Times* newspaper, before becoming an English professor at King's College, London. He is best known for his translations and publications of ancient Scandinavian folk and fairy stories.

BROTHERS GRIMM
Jacob Ludwig Karl Grimm 1785~1863
Wilhelm Karl Grimm 1786~1859

Jacob and Wilhelm Grimm were born near Frankfurt, Germany. They read law at university, but were inspired to study how spoken language changes over time. This led them to collect many popular oral European folk tales and set them down on paper. Jacob did most of the research while Wilhelm did more of the writing.

JOSEPH JACOBS 1854–1916

Joseph Jacobs was born in Australia. As a young man he studied in England and Germany, researching Jewish history, before settling in America. He was inspired by the Brothers Grimm to take an interest in folklore and edited five collections of fairy tales: *English Fairy Tales*, *More English Fairy Tales*, *Celtic Fairy Tales*, *More Celtic Fairy Tales*, and *European Folk and Fairy Tales*.

ANDREW LANG 1844–1912

Andrew Lang was born in Selkirk, Scotland, and studied at St Andrew's and Oxford Universities. He researched folklore, mythology, and religion, and wrote poetry, novels and literary criticism. Andrew is best known as the collector and reteller of twelve books of folk and fairy tales for children.

YEI THEODORA OZAKI 1871–1933

Yei Theodora Ozaki was born into nobility, to a British mother and a Japanese father, Baron Ozaki. She married Yukio Ozaki, the Mayor of Tokyo, who was influential in international politics. Her lifelong passion was collecting and retelling ancient Japanese folk tales.

FLORA ANNIE STEEL 1847–1929

Spending 22 years living in India, Flora Annie Steel involved herself in all sorts of projects, which included acting as a school inspector and collecting local folklore.

KATE DOUGLAS WIGGIN 1856–1923
NORA ARCHIBALD SMITH 1859–1934

Kate Douglas Wiggin and Nora Archibald Smith were sisters, born in Philadelphia. Kate started the first free kindergarten in San Francisco. She and Nora then established a training school for kindergarten teachers, and raised money by writing children's stories. Nora also wrote academic essays on the education and welfare of children. Together they gathered, retold, and edited many collections of tales for children.

About the Artists

SI CLARK   Si spends the majority of his time drawing and is more than a little obsessed with it. After graduating from Bournemouth, UK, in 2005, he moved to London where he has been developing his illustration style and also working in different fields, such as animation, design, and typography.

The Master and His Pupil, Rapunzel, Childe Rowland, Tamlane, The Prince and the Dragon, The Sprightly Tailor, The Snow Queen, The Devil and his Grandmother, Little Red Riding Hood, The Jelly Fish and the Monkey

PETER COTTRILL   As well as illustrating books, Peter does some teaching and practises Shiatsu. He enjoys creating stories and scenarios. Humor and a sense of the absurd inspire Peter. Throw in some costumes and wild animals and he's even happier. For Peter, a brief is a chance to be creative and see what he can come up with, whatever the subject.

Aladdin and the Wonderful Lamp, The Wicked Witch of the West, The Dragon of the North, The History of Jack the Giant-Killer, Tom Tit Tot, Mr Miacca, The Rose Tree, The Singing Bone, Schippeitaro

LUKE FINLAYSON   Luke enrolled at a 2D animation school over ten years ago, and studied for three years before working on various animated shows. He later turned to illustration and wrote his first fairy tale, *Lily of the Valley*, which he is currently illustrating. Luke has a great love of illustration and stories of wild imagination, and he is captivated and inspired by fairy tales.

The Little Mermaid, Hansel and Grettel, The Demon with the Matted Hair, The Third Voyage of Sinbad the Sailor, The Gifts of the Little People, The Goblin of Adachigahara, The King who would see Paradise, Mr Fox, Beauty and the Beast

GERALD KELLEY   Gerald works from his illustration studio in Florida. Originally working in watercolor and pencil, he is now working completely digitally, from initial sketches to final highlights. Arthur Rackham and Edmund Dulac are two major inspirations for his decision to work as an illustrator. Gerald can be found huddled over his drawing screen and talking to his Border Collie, Scout.

The Witch, The Horned Women, Rushen Coatie, The Twelve Brothers, The Story of the Fisherman, The Ogre of Rashomon, The Red Shoes, The Ratcatcher, The Farmer and the Badger, The Strange Visitor

DUNCAN SMITH   After graduating from the Glasgow School of Art, Duncan moved to London to work as an illustrator. He works in both traditional and digital mediums, but his favorite is watercolors. Duncan has a love of drawing the human figure. His work has been published worldwide and he is also the author of six children's books.

How Bradamante Conquered the Wizard, The Mandarin and the Butterfly, The Terrible Head, Jorinda and Jorindel, Tritill, Litill, and the Birds, Bluebeard, Gold-tree and Silver-tree, Boots and the Troll, The Goblin Pony